I0547610

DEVIL'S LAKE

CHARLES RAY

North Potomac, MD

Devil's Lake is a work of fiction. Names, descriptions, places, and incidents are products of the author's imagination, or are used fictionally. Any resemblance to actual events or persons, living or dead, is purely coincidental.

The reproduction or distribution, by any means, including electronic distribution, is expressly prohibited without the written consent of the copyright holder, except for fair use quotes in connection with reviews.

For information about this and other works of this author, contact the author at charlesray.author@gmail.com.

For a complete listing of the author's work, check out his Amazon Author Page at http://www.amazon.com/Charles-Ray/e/B006WMLEZK

Cover photo and design by the author

Author's photo by Denise Ray-Wickersham

Printed in the United States of America.

Uhuru Press, North Potomac, MD

Copyright © 2016 Charles Ray

All rights reserved.

ISBN: 0692644555
ISBN-13: 978-0692644553

For my grandchildren, Samantha, Catherine, and Thomas. You're too young to read this now, but someday . . . someday.

CHAPTER 1

The room was large, much longer than it was wide, and colored almost entirely in light beige, nearly of white, marble. Floor, walls and ceiling were all the same, the ceiling's pattern broken only by the four banks of fluorescent lights spaced equidistantly from front to rear and bathing the space in a soft yellowish glow, the floor only by the barely visible swirls of a color only slightly darker, and the walls by narrow, floor-to-ceiling recesses every six feet. The entrance was a large blond wooden door, curved at the top, set in the center of the wall. Upon entering, one could see, fifty feet away at the far end of the room, a dark shape, straight on three sides, curved at the top, jet black, but not shiny, the bottom of which was three feet from the floor. Soft music played from speakers that were discretely concealed somewhere in the walls. The air in the room was neither warm, nor cold, and there was a slight flowery odor in the air that flowed gently, moved about by a ventilation system that was absolutely silent.

Two men, one light brown skinned with piercing, but sad brown eyes and dark brown hair brushed straight back on his oval skull causing it to ripple like gentle ocean waves, and one with a ruddy complexion, deep blue eyes, and blond hair that resisted neatness and order no matter how much he brushed it. Both were dressed in black suits, with pearl colored shirts, and blood-red, almost black, ties. They were the same height, but the blond was a few pounds heavier. The blond rested a hand on his friend's shoulder.

"Is there anything you need right now, Brad?" he asked.

"No, Bill," the other man said, placing a slender brown hand over the other's sun tanned hand. "I'll be okay. Thanks for coming, though."

Tears sprang into the blond's eyes. "Hey, the Three Musketeers have to stick together," he said quietly. His lips quivered, and then he began crying.

The other man pulled him into an embrace. "It's okay, Bill. She's gone to a better place. At least now she's not suffering anymore."

Bradley Matthews, age 32, and William Lewis, age 33, had been friends and classmates since meeting at freshman orientation when they entered Georgetown

University ten years earlier. The third Musketeer, Lena Matthews, nee Nelson, had been at that same orientation. She was also present – in a manner of speaking – in the marble room.

The room was the main hall of Eternal Rest Funeral Home and Crematorium, and Bradley and William had come there on this warm April morning for the cremation of Lena, Bradley's wife and William's friend, who had died three days earlier – on April 1 – from the pancreatic cancer that had been eating away at her insides for nine months. Lena had been 32, three months younger than Bradley, when she died.

There had been only the two of them, not counting of course the staff of the establishment, at the memorial service. Bradley had insisted. The three of them had no family, and he had no wish to subject himself to the somber condolences of faculty members from the university with whom he'd spoken no more than a dozen words during the entire time he'd worked as a creative writing instructor there.

Lack of family had, in fact, been what had drawn the three of them together in the first place. They'd been thrown together during freshman orientation. The incoming students had been grouped alphabetically. Bradley Matthews, William Lewis, and Lena Nelson found themselves seated together near the back of the room where they were the only three with last names beginning with the letters L through O. Bradley and William had learned that they were both orphans; Bradley had been abandoned by his unwed mother right after birth, and had spent his entire life in a series of orphanages and foster homes, and William's parents had been killed in a boating accident when he was eight. He too had spent his years growing up in one foster home after another. Lena, had sat quietly near them until the break when she noticed the two of them huddled in a corner avoiding the rest of the incoming freshman class. She walked over and introduced herself. Neither Brad nor William had until that time had much experience with the opposite sex, and she was without doubt the most beautiful woman to ever speak to them, so she quickly became a part of the group. A few days after meeting her, they learned that she too had been orphaned – when she was twelve, her parents had died in an auto crash coming back from an art auction in southwestern Virginia. She had been sleeping on the back seat when they ran off the road and into a large tree, which was the only thing that saved her. Neither of her parents had siblings and she too wound up in foster care until a distant cousin learned of her plight and took her in. This, though, was enough to establish an unbreakable bond among the three, who soon began calling themselves the Three Musketeers. Somewhere about their junior year, a bond closer than friendship manifested itself between Bradley and Lena. William, who had experienced a strengthening of feeling for Lena himself, the good friend that he was, took losing out to Bradley as only a true friend would. He wished them the best, served as best man at the wedding, and had been almost a part of their family until the day she died.

"What are your plans now?" William asked.

"I haven't really given it a lot of thought." Bradley shook his head. His eyes glistened, but he'd been unable to cry. "I always let Lena make the decisions, you know. She was good at that."

"You know you can always count on me if you need anything."

Bradley put a hand on William's shoulder, squeezing gently. "I know, man," he said quietly. "I know."

As the two friends stood there then, in silence, each thinking his own thoughts about what they had lost, a tall, gaunt man, dressed in a black suit, the coat of which came nearly to his knees, with his thin black hair pomaded and plastered to his egg-shaped head, a sharp nose that threatened to curve down into his thin lips, and skin the color of egg shells, came from a door in the front wall that was invisible until it opened. In his hands he carried a plain metal urn, golden colored, narrow at the top. He came to a stop in front of Bradley, a look of commiseration on his pasty face.

"Mr. Matthews," he said in a voice that sounded as if he was speaking through thick gauze. "Please do accept the deepest condolences from all of us here at Eternal Rest for your loss."

Bradley stared, first at the man, and then at the urn he proffered. He had trouble focusing his eyes and attention. The man made a soft coughing sound in the back of his throat which shook Bradley out of his fugue. He slowly reached for the urn, which the man deposited gently into his grip. When he was sure that Bradley had control, he removed his hands, bowed slightly and turned on his heels and silently glided across the marble floor to the invisible door that again opened revealing a dark space beyond into which he disappeared like the phantom he appeared to Bradley and William to be.

The two friends looked into each other's eyes, searching for some words, but nothing came. William was afraid to speak, for fear he would start crying again. He knew that public displays of emotion upset Bradley. Bradley, for his part, wanted to thank his friend for standing by him at this time, but the words seemed to stick in his throat. He cradled the urn to his chest. He *had* to say something. Lena would have expected it. In fact, he thought, at this point she would be nudging him in the side and making faces at him in an effort to goad him into speaking. The thought almost brought a smile to his lips, but when as he thought of her, he felt as if his heart would shatter into tiny pieces and explode from his chest. He took slow, deep breaths to calm his mind. Finally, he looked into his friend's eyes.

"Well, I guess it's time to take her home," he said quietly.

Without waiting for William to respond, he turned and started for the exit, his shoes making whispering sounds on the marble floor.

Charles Ray

CHAPTER 2

Bradley pushed open the door and entered the tiny living room of the red-brick row house on Thirty-Third Street, a few blocks east of Georgetown University campus. He stopped just inside the door, momentarily at a loss as to what to do next. The quiet was unsettling, unnerving, seeming to press down on him. Not that it had ever been a noisy place. Lena never let him play the radio loud, claiming that it would upset the neighbors. But, there had at least been the sound of her voice, singing as she prepared supper, or the whispering sound of her slippers on the hardwood floors.

He stood there, staring across the room at the fireplace, and the photos of the two of them on the mantle. Tears began to flow, unbidden, over his cheeks.

"Oh, God, I'm going to miss you," he said. He began to sob. "What will I do without you?"

But, she could no longer answer him. No longer would she walk across the room when he was depressed, and rub his shoulders or kiss the curly hair on top of his head.

He walked to the center of the room, a total of four steps from the tiny entryway, stopped and let his hand run along the back of the old sofa they'd bought from the goodwill store when they first bought the house and only had a limited budget for furniture. The fluffy brown upholstery had more hairballs than a kennel full of cats, and didn't fit with anything else in the room, but they'd become so attached to it, it retained the place of honor in the room. The off-white lace doilies Lena had made during her 'learn to croquet' phase still draped slightly off center over the arms. He sat at the end of the sofa nearest the door and cradled the urn against his chest, looking down at the doilies with their slightly off kilter stitches. He'd kidded her about it at first, but she'd stuck to her guns and insisted they be used. Not one of their friends who'd visited them had noticed—or mentioned—the odd stitching, and he'd come to love the silly things almost as much as he loved her.

He ran a finger over the edge of one of the doilies, conjuring up an image of her sitting on his lap as he did so. She would be nuzzling her head into the hollow of his shoulder, and he'd be breathing in the lemony smell of shampoo in her soft, black hair. A shudder coursed through him at the thought.

With a sigh, he heaved himself up from the sofa and walked to the fireplace. He placed the urn on the mantle next to the photo they'd had some Japanese tourist take of them on a visit to Ocean City the year before her cancer had been detected during a routine physical examination. They were leaning in with their arms around each other, smiling at the camera as if they didn't have a care in the world—and, at that time they didn't. The cares were to come later when the doctor said he'd spotted a suspicious shadow on Lena's x-ray, and wanted to do some follow-up tests. When the results of those tests came back, Bradley's world broke into a million tiny shards of hopelessness. The cancer had advanced to a point where surgery wasn't recommended, and despite aggressive chemotherapy and radiation treatments it continued to advance.

He tried to block the memory of her last minutes, lying frail and shrunken in a hospital bed hooked up to monitors with tubes feeding painkillers into her system to ease the almost unbearable pain she'd suffered the last few days of her life. Her passing was quiet. Bradley hadn't noticed when the sheet over her shrunken breasts stopped rising and falling. It was the shrill sound of the monitors when she flat-lined that told him she was gone.

He picked up the picture, running his forefinger over the glass. Two such different people they were; he could hardly believe that they were so good together. Her, with her porcelain complexion, hair so black it had blue highlights, bright green eyes that were always smiling, and with her hair in a modified Pageboy cut, a pixie-like appearance that made her look ten years younger than she was. He, on the other hand, with his caramel colored skin and close cropped brown hair, and dark brown eyes that never smiled, looked five years older. He was smiling in the photo, but anyone looking close enough would see the lack of a smile in his eyes. He had been happy—with her—but, there was always that tinge of sadness lurking in the back of his thoughts, the sense of not belonging that had come from being bounced from one foster home to another, finally ending up in an orphanage in Frederick County, Maryland, just outside the town of Frederick until he turned eighteen and won the scholarship to attend Georgetown, fortunately, all expenses paid, which meant moving from the orphanage to a dormitory.

Standing there, he let his forehead rest against the cool stone of the mantle. One salty tear seeped from the corner of his eye and rolled slowly down his left cheek. He stifled a sob that began deep in his chest. Then, he pulled away. Everywhere he turned in the room her presence was there. He strode quickly from the living room, through a smaller dining nook, into the kitchen. Even here he felt her presence. Not as heavily as in the rest of the house, for they ate out a lot, but it was there.

He opened the cabinet and took out the white porcelain tea kettle, filled it with water from the sink and sat it on the stove. While the water was heating, he took a packet of jasmine tea from the counter drawer and put it in a Dallas Cowboys' mug. Soon, the tea kettle was making a whistling noise. He took it from the burner and poured a stream of steaming water over the tea bag.

When the liquid in the mug had turned the color of dark mahogany he removed the tea bag and dropped it in the trash can near the sink. He then moved to the oil-cloth draped square table in the corner next to the stove, pulled out a chair and sat, looking out of the flyspeck-dotted window glass at the tiny back yard, packed from corner to corner of the six-foot high fence with the detritus of a young couple who, when they did entertain at home and the weather was nice, preferred the outdoors. An old grill they'd bought at a garage sale, once green, but now mostly the red of rust; a picnic table that one had to crawl over to get to the gate—a chore when lugging the garbage container to be put out for weekly pickup—and only had three useable sides for that same reason; and a croquet set laid out in a modified pattern because the dimensions of the leftover space in the yard didn't permit the traditional layout. He cupped the mug in his hands, feeling the warmth through the thick ceramic sides, and thinking about the last time they'd sat at that table.

It was the fourth of July, with the moisture-laden heat that seemed to press down on you like a heavy wool blanket. Despite that, he and Lena had decided to have a July 4th cookout in the backyard, to which they'd invited their best friend, Bill, along with his current girlfriend, Agatha, a tall, slim, blonde with out of control bangs that constantly covered her light blue eyes. She'd shown up wearing a halter top that barely contained her breasts—large for her slim frame—and showed her flat stomach down to just below her navel, and a pair of shorts that were so tight they looked painted on. He worried that Lena would be offended by the woman's dress, or lack thereof, but in true Lena style, she had merely taken the blonde by the arm and led her out to the backyard, chatting at her like she'd known her forever.

He pulled Bill aside as the two women exited the kitchen.

"Bill, where the hell did you find that?" he asked, a note of tension in his voice.

His old friend laughed and punched his shoulder playfully. "Don't sweat it, Brad," he said. "She just looks like a bimbo. Actually, she's a corporate lawyer. Works for one of the big lobbying firms down on K Street. I figured it was a summer cookout, so casual attire is appropriate, right?"

They had specified casual in the invitation, but Bradley knew that Lena's idea of casual meant the tasteful mid-thigh shorts and sleeveless blouse she was wearing; clothing that showed off her figure without actually putting most of it on display.

"I guess it's okay," he said. "Lena doesn't seem to mind."

"Hey, after a few drinks, no one will notice," Bill said.

"Uh, Lena and I won't be drinking much. We're doing our physical exams in a few days and thought it'd be a good idea to let the booze leach from our systems, you know."

Bill laughed that hearty 'all is well with the world' laugh that Bradley knew so well.

"You two are so anal retentive. You need to learn to loosen up and go with the flow a little more. Nothing you drink today's gonna be in your system that long."

Bradley knew that, but there was something else he and Lena had been discussing, and he wondered if he should share it with his friend—their friend.

"Well, if you promise to keep that big mouth of yours shut about it," he said. "There's another reason we're cutting back on alcohol."

For a brief moment a look of worry flickered across Bill Lewis's face. "You're not sick are you?"

Bradley laughed. "No, it's nothing like that. Look you have to promise me you won't say anything, and that you won't let Lena know I told you."

"Cross my heart and hope to die, stick a finger in my eye. Now, spill!"

"We're planning on having a baby."

"Wha-, a baby . . . you're kidding, right? No, you're not kidding. Wow! I get to be an uncle. I am gonna be the godfather, right? When? Come on, man, spill."

Bradley held his hands up in surrender.

"Whoa, pardner," he said. "We've still got the mechanical part to get past, and then a nine-month wait after that, but don't worry, we wouldn't have anyone else as the godfather. First, we want to get thorough checkups, you know, to make sure everything's in working order, and since the University health plan pays for a physical exam every year, we figured we might as well kill two birds with one stone."

"Wow! You two with a kid. I mean, that's so rad! Wow!"

"Remember now, you promised to keep your mouth shut."

"I will never utter a word."

And, he hadn't. Not even when he'd learned later that the doctor had discovered Lena's cancer during the examination. Not once during the funeral ceremony and cremation. Bradley knew that Bill had been as devastated by events as he had. The three of them had bonded during four years of college, becoming the family none had ever really had before. And now, one third of that family, the part that was greater than the other two, the part that held them together . . . was gone.

Everywhere he looked she was there. Except that . . . she wasn't there. She would never be there again.

He wanted to go upstairs, get in bed and pull the covers over his head. But, he wouldn't do that. He hadn't done that since she went into the hospital. When he wasn't dozing fitfully on the hard chair near her bed, he was curled up on the sofa—the only way his six foot frame could fit on the three-cushion monstrosity. And, even there her presence made itself felt. The scent of her shampoo as he nuzzled her hair, the lavender smell of the soap she used when she showered, it was on everything, everwhere he turned it was there. But, *she* wasn't there. Sometimes, when he walked from one room to another, he'd stop and look around, as if expecting to see her standing just around the corner of the door, or walking up behind him. Then, he'd curse himself, because he knew she wouldn't.

I have to get out of here, he thought. Not because I want to forget her, but because I want to mourn her without the constant pull of reminders that she's not here. It made no sense, even as he thought it. He should *want* to have things around to remind him of her, but he didn't. All he wanted was the images he had in his mind. With that he could process the loss. That was what one part of his mind told him. I have to get away. I have to get away. Get away. Get away. The voice was insistent. It would not stop until he heeded its chant. Get away.

He rose from the table, leaving the mug with its now cool contents, and walked into the living room like a sleepwalker. Straight to the corner table near the fireplace. He picked up the phone.

CHAPTER 3

The island was a small hummock of land, *a lopsided circle about twenty feet in diameter, covered with white oak, beech and maple trees draped in moss and English ivy. Four feet above the level of the lake at its highest point, its edges slid into the murky water that lapped quietly against the mossy black earth. Not that anyone could see that, because the island was shrouded in a perpetual mist that undulated, waved, and billowed in an inverted cup that surrounded the island, reaching out over the lake ten feet from the rim of the island and hovering ten feet above it like a diaphanous dome.*

The lake, which the lake sat in the center of, was shaped like a partially deflated football, a mile long from point to point, and three-quarters of a mile across at its widest point. Locally it was known as Devil's Lake, and it sat just south of a small town Copper Cove. No one remembered why the lake was called Devil's Lake or why the town was named Copper Cove, for as far as anyone knew the devil didn't live anywhere in the area, and there were no mountains, only a thickly wooded forest of pine, oak, walnut, birch and assorted other trees, that surrounded it and grew right up to the two-lane blacktop that ran through the center, and not a gram of copper around except in the ancient pipes in the structures that lined that blacktop.

The population of Copper Cove was 200 people, give or take. No one bothered to keep close records. It was a quiet town, as quiet as the small graveyard behind the tiny church, with its ten headstones leaning every which way and colored grey and green with age; so corroded and covered with mold the names and dates could no longer be read. The people walking the uneven sidewalks nodded at each other rather than speak. Even the antiquated vehicles, cars from the 50s and 60s, ran quietly, when they ran at all.

It liked it that way. The quiet. In its home deep in the thick trees of the forest on the island, the only sounds were the lapping of the water on the shore of the island and the soft murmur of the wind blowing through the trees.

While the quiet was desired, it was uneasy. The energy that kept it alive was . . . waning. It could feel it slowly ebbing away, bit by bit, sucking away its very essence. The source of energy was weakening. For the first time in oh so very long it was beginning to feel depleted, deflated, diminished. To be exiled in this strange place had been punishment enough, had it not? Being ripped away from others of its kind and left to languish in this alien place was sufficient penitence for what were after all merely misdemeanors in the cosmic scheme. But, to be deprived of energy meant the end of existence, a punishment out of proportion to the crime—or so it believed. If indeed belief was a cognitive process that could be applied to it.

So, it reasoned, this must have been the plan all along. Exile was not the ultimate intent of being transported to this despicable backwater. Oh no. That was just a preliminary to the true objective. Annihilation. The plan all along had been to lull it into a false sense of security and then snuff it out of existence. How could it have been so naïve? It was not the crime itself that was serious it was the temerity it had displayed in even contemplating the commission that had so infuriated them. Of course they would destroy it. They would never rest until it was no longer because they feared it.

And, well they should. For, despite its love for solitude, or rather, its ability to endure solitude, it had not been idle. It could not move what remained of its corporeal form beyond the perimeter of the island—it could not travel over water, could, in fact, not bear contact with the noxious substance. But, it could influence events and entities beyond its liquid prison

It knew the reason for the decline in energy

inputs. And, it knew the answer to reversing that decline. It had but to reach out and find a new source. And, reach out it had, sending its tendrils in all directions until it found what it sought. And, then, it had set in motion the events required to place this new source of energy where it would be most useful. Soon, very soon, it would have what it needed, and if the plan it had set in motion worked as it was confident it would, it would have more than just what it needed, it would have what it had long wanted—a way off the damned island.

CHAPTER 4

Professor Rebecca Davis adjusted the hem of her skirt, pulling it as far over her knees as she could. When she first sat down behind the transparent glass sheet on an aluminum frame that she called a desk, Bradley had gotten a good view of the terrain beneath her brown skirt, several inches of creamy thighs. She had extremely nice legs for a woman approaching fifty, but he felt guilty ogling her so soon after Lena's death, so he'd looked down at his hands clasped tightly on the tops of his thighs and hoped she hadn't noticed.

He'd gotten through to her on Saturday—unlike many of the other professors she gave her staff her cell phone number in case of an emergency—and made an appointment to see her first thing on Monday. First thing turned out to be 9:00 am, giving him an hour before her first lecture on 'Comedy-The Dying American Art Form,' which she taught to freshmen enrolled in the Department of

English and Comparative Literature. She was the assistant dean of the department, and specialized in creative writing and film, and supervised Bradley who taught a course in 'Introduction to Fiction.'

They met in her office, only a bit larger than his, but with a significantly greater number of certificates and diplomas on her walls, and several first edition books in the bookcase behind her desk.

"Okay, Bradley," she said after she was satisfied that her skirt met whatever standards of decorum and decency she applied to such matters. "What is so urgent that you had to see me before my first class?"

Davis, though easy going in many things with the instructors—she refused to call them professors until they'd defended their theses and been awarded their doctorates— she was something of a harridan when it came to having her teaching schedule interfered with. She never, never before this day that is, saw anyone before her first scheduled class of the day, and never spoke to students outside her established office hours.

"Uh, I'm sorry Dr. Davis," he said, feeling like a truant who has been sent in to see the vice principal. "It is important, you might even say urgent, or I wouldn't have bothered you on a Saturday like I did."

She turned in her swivel chair, thrusting her legs out, causing her skirt to hike up again, revealing even more thigh than she had when he first entered, and steepling her well-manicured fingers in front of her face. She looked at him over the tips of her fingers and pursed her thin lips. Bradley couldn't be sure if the expression he saw in her amber eyes was compassion or anger. It was often hard to tell with Davis.

"I, uh, we all are so sorry for you loss," she said. "Lena was a wonderful person who will be sorely missed. I know you must be absolutely devastated at the moment, and I assumed you'd like a few days off to grieve properly."

He was surprised that she'd remembered Lena's name. They'd only met, what, maybe three times, and as far as Bradley knew had never had a conversation. But, then, Lena was like that. She made an impression on everyone she met. They remembered her. He wondered if they felt the hollowness caused by her absent as strongly as he did.

"Yes, I thank you for that, and that's what I wanted to talk to you about."

Davis flipped back a stray lock of her blonde hair that had draped over her left eye.

"What, your grief or your time off?"

"Time off," he said. "You said I could take a week, but I think I'm going to need more than that."

Now, her eyes, which had been wide with . . . sympathy . . . narrowed.

"And, just how much additional time do

you think you need?"

Bradley steeled himself. He knew well that what he was about to say would not be received well. He had classroom commitments that would have to be covered by one of the other PhD candidates, or heaven forbid, one of the tenured professors. But, he also knew that if he didn't do it he was likely to go quietly crazy.

"I think I need to get away for a good long while, Dr. Davis. I was thinking maybe the next year?"

Her eyes went wide. "A . . . year! You can't be serious. We can't cover your absence for an entire year."

"I know it's an imposition," he said. "And, I hate to ask, but I simply *must* get away for a while."

"I could handle it if it was just your fiction class." She slowly shook her head. "But, we're introducing a new class on 'Introduction to Writing' in the fall, and I was planning on having you teach it."

Bradley sat back in his chair, shocked. Teach a completely new class in fall, and here it was April and she was just now telling him. He'd be busy twelve to fourteen hours a day until September, doing his current classes and creating a syllabus. He'd thought before that she cared for her subordinates, but this put a new light on things.

"It would have been nice of you to tell me this before now," he said. "I truly am sorry, but I just can't do it. I have to get away. If I don't, I'll . . ."

Davis leaned forward. Her scooped blouse billowed out allowing Bradley a fulsome view of her more than ample breasts. She licked her top lip and smiled.

"I'm truly sorry for your loss, Bradley," she said in a low voice. "But, running away won't help. It won't bring Lena back." She rolled her chair forward until she was at the edge of her desk and her knees were millimeters from his. He could feel the heat of her body through his jeans. "Look, we can work this out, Bradley, truly we can. Why don't you take a month, no two months off, and then come back and we can see where it goes." She put her hand on his knees. "You're one of my best lecturers, Bradley. The department won't be the same if you're gone."

He didn't like the way she said that. His plan was to be gone for a year, maybe two. But, then, he could see the problem. His problems notwithstanding, it was hardly fair to expect the university to hold his position open for one year much less two. Davis, though, was sending mixed signals. On the one hand, her voice was saying that if he took off, he was toast, but the other hand, resting gently on his thigh now, was saying something else entirely.

His mind was a tangle, knotted like a ball of yarn after a kitten's swatted it around for hours.

The pressure on his thigh increased. "Please, Bradley," she said. "At least promise me you'll give it some consideration. Go home, sleep on it, and call me in the morning. I'll have one of the other PhD's cover your classes for the rest of the semester. I . . . we need you here. You know that, don't you?"

"I . . . I don't know what to say, Dr. Davis, I—"

She patted his thigh. "Look, we've been working together long enough that we're beyond titles. Please, Bradley, call me Rebecca. You know, your dissertation defense is scheduled soon, and I have no doubt you'll pass with flying colors. You'll soon be Dr. Bradley Matthews, or Professor Matthews, so you might as well get accustomed to being my equal."

"Thanks, Dr. Da-, er, Rebecca," he said. "Okay, I'll go home and think on it some more. I have to be fair and warn you, though, I don't think I'll change my mind."

He left her sitting there. She seemed to be lost in thought, just staring at him without expression and unaware that her skirt had hiked up past mid-thigh, exposing the hot pink underwear she wore.

CHAPTER 5

"No shit, she really flashed her tits and crotch at you?" William Lewis clapped Bradley's shoulder and stared open-mouthed at him. "You're yankin' my chain, right? I mean, Davis is a fine lookin' broad for her age, but . . . you think she was comin' on to you? Really?"

Bradley blinked. He wasn't sure what had happened. He was, in fact, so confused by his encounter with Rebecca Davis, rather than going back home, he'd hailed a cab on Thirty-Fifth Street, just outside Georgetown's campus, and taken it to his friend's condo near Virginia Avenue not far from the old Watergate Complex. It was, to Bradley's dismay, very close to George Washington University, the Protestant response to Catholic Georgetown, and a sprawling urban university that was eating up most of the real estate east of the Watergate. Bill had maintained that it was more convenient than living in the Georgetown area since he worked as an analyst—Bradley and Lena had never fully understood what it was he analyzed—for a big lobbying firm on K Street, just east of Washington Circle, just over a mile from his condo, saving him on transportation costs and allowing him to get exercise through his twice daily walking commute to and from work. Bradley knew that it was also because it gave his horny friend access to the coeds of GWU and the lonely secretaries of the nearby State Department. While he'd been confused by Rebecca Davis's actions, Bill, as usual, had gone straight to the most carnal interpretation possible.

"I don't know," he said. "She might just have been trying to convince me not to take too much time off. Just as I was leaving, she actually let her skirt slide up enough for me to see her panties. They were hot pink."

"Yeah, and she had to flash her snatch and rub your crotch to do that . . . get you to take less time off?"

Bradley felt his cheeks flame. His friend, with his crude sense of humor and absolute lack of discretion, had always had a way of doing that, and without Lena around to rein him in he was incorrigible.

"She didn't do either. . . well, she didn't rub my crotch," he protested. "She just touched the top of my leg."

"But, you know what I mean. Hell, she's a PhD, *and* your boss, if she wanted you to take less time off, why didn't she just come out and say it?"

"Uh, er, well, I guess she didn't want to appear bossy. You know how it is. If a woman supervisor is too direct, she's called bitchy."

"So, what *are* you gonna do?" William also had a way of changing subjects at supersonic speed, moving from one topic to another without bothering to achieve closure, and without warning.

"About what?" Bradley asked.

"Why, taking time off, of course. What'd you think I meant?"

Bradley shrugged in answer to both questions. He wasn't sure now what he should do, and he hadn't understood what his friend meant.

"What do you think I should do?"

William got up, went into the small kitchen just off the living room, and took two Budweisers from the refrigerator. He popped the tab on one and took a long, loud drink. Then, he came back into the living room and tossed the unopened can to Bradley.

"What should you do? Damn, dude," he said. "That's a good question. What do you *want* to do?"

"I want to be at home, holding a warm and living   Lena   in   my   arms," is what Bradley wanted to say, but instead he said, "I want the hurt to go away. I want not to feel so much emptiness inside me. That's what I want to do."

Blunt he might be. His language was crude. But, William Lewis was Bradley Matthews' best friend, had been since they met in freshman orientation, and he knew when his friend was hurting. He put his almost empty can down and laid a hand gently on Bradley's shoulder.

"Hey, dude," he said. "You gotta do what makes you feel better. Screw the school, screw Davis . . . and I mean that figuratively in this case . . . just go for what eases your pain. If that department of hers is so weak it can't deal with you not being there for a while, you probably shouldn't be there at all, know what I mean?"

"Yeah, I do know what you mean, and you're right."

"The department's that screwed up?"

Bradley laughed for the first time in months. "No, although, now that you mention it, it probably is, I mean you're right when you say I have to start thinking for myself."

CHAPTER 6

Three people, two men and a woman, sat at a large oak table in a nondescript room in the back of a nondescript building. The only light in the room came from a single bulb suspended from the rafters above what would have been the ceiling, if there had been a ceiling. The walls of the room were bare, and except for the table and three chairs, the room was bare of furniture.

The woman sat on one of the long sides of the table near the center, facing the two men who sat across from her. She leaned forward, brushing a lock of raven hair from in front of her ice blue eyes as she did so. Both men leaned back as if avoiding her banging into them, despite the four feet of table that separated them.

"He is getting impatient," she said. Her voice was deep and resonant, without a trace of warmth. "When will the . . . when will he arrive?"

The two men shared a nervous glance. The one on the woman's right, a narrow faced man with wheat colored hair combed straight back from his high forehead and prominent ears, tugged at the collar of his khaki shirt, and brushed absently at the gold badge over his left breast pocket.

"Uh, we don't have a definite arrival time," he said. He swallowed hard. "I'm pretty sure it won't be more than a few more days, though."

The other man, shorter, heavier, with dark brown hair and a severely receding hairline, brushed his hand across his forehead.

"Yes, no more than a few days, surely," he said.

"He is reaching the end of his patience," she said. "He is tired of waiting. I am not sure how much longer I can convince him to wait."

Khaki shirt leaned forward. A deep frown creased his face. "What does he expect us to do?"

She leaned forward, spearing him with an icy blue glare.

"*He* expects *you* to do what you are told." Her tone was as icy as her stare. "And, he will not accept excuses."

The short, heavyset man made a noise between a puff and a snort. "All we were told is that we were to bring him here, but we weren't told how or why," he said.

"It is your job to figure out *how*," she said, glaring at him. "As to why, you do not need to know."

The venom in her voice caused both men to push back from the table. Their faces went pale, and beads of sweat popped out on their foreheads.

"We mean no harm by asking," the narrow faced man said. "It just makes it much easier to do a job when you have some understanding about the reason for doing it."

"The reason you are doing it is simple," she said. "You are doing it because he wants you to do it, just as you have always done what he wants you to do. Or is that no longer sufficient for you?"

Both men were now shaking as if suffering some illness. Their eyes were wide and their pupils dilated.

"No, no, certainly not," they said in unison.

"We will, of course, do as you say," the fat man said. "It is just . . . going out there is very disturbing."

The woman smiled and sat back in her chair.

"Yes, I suppose it is. Very well, you are forgiven . . . this time. Just make sure you do not ever question your orders, ever again."

She did not have to raise a hand, move her head, or say anything. They knew they were dismissed. Both men stood and nearly tripped each other in their haste to leave the room.

Long after their departure, she sat there, her eyes narrow slits, looking at the wall in front of her, humming quietly, seeing nothing. Then, her eyes snapped open, and she stood.

"Yes, right away," she said to the empty room. "It will be as you wish."

"We must be right this time," a threatening voice echoed in the woman's head, causing her to tremble.

CHAPTER 7

Bradley spent two days thinking about what Rebecca Davis and his friend Bill had said to him. Two days, mostly lying on his back on the bed he'd shared with Lena, staring at the ceiling, counting the imperfections in the plaster, getting up only to go to the bathroom or fix a sandwich.

Finally, on Thursday, he decided what he was going to do.

It was five in the morning, and he'd been lying there feeling sorry for himself, unable to sleep, when he decided first that he was hungry. Not just that waking up for the first time desire for a small breakfast kind of hunger, either. What he had was a clean out the pantry, empty the refrigerator, I could eat a cow, hide and all hunger, that clawed at his gut like a kitten trying to escape from a burlap bag because it knows it's on a one-way trip to the river.

Rather than keep lying there bemoaning his fate, he rolled from the bed as if someone had tilted it. In the bathroom, he relieved the pressure on his bladder and the brick in his bowel, brushed his teeth shaved, took a shower, and spent a little extra time brushing his short, wiry hair until it lay in relatively tidy waves.

After donning a pair of faded jeans and a Dallas Cowboys' polo shirt, he pulled a pair of brown loafers over his bare feet, made the bed, and went into the tiny kitchen.

From the refrigerator he took two eggs, a week-old carton of milk, a package of bacon from the crisper, a stick of butter from the little bin in the door, and a loaf of whole wheat bread, and put them on the counter between the stovetop and the microwave. From the pantry he took two medium sized white potatoes and a small onion. He then took two plastic plates from the cabinet over the sink.

Preparing breakfast was one of the few things Lena would allow him to do in the kitchen, complaining that even though he was a good cook he left the place so messy it took her an hour to clean up.

"Well, I'll show you," he said to himself. "This morning, I'll leave this place so clean you could eat right off the counter."

He half expected her to come up silently behind him and put her hands over his eyes and say something silly, and stifled a moan when he remembered that she would never be doing that again.

"Maybe that's the first sign of going crazy," he said again to the window over the sink. "Talking to someone who is not there."

To take his mind off what he was beginning to think was a deteriorating state of mind he began the methodical and mechanical process of preparing breakfast, reminding himself as he worked not to prepare for two.

He stuck two slices of bread into the toaster, and began peeling the potatoes and onions. After putting the peels in the trash can beneath the counter, he diced the potatoes and onions and mixed dumped them into a plastic bowl. To this mixture he added salt, black pepper, garlic powder and some barbecue powder and mixed it all up. He then heated a tablespoon of vegetable oil in a deep skillet, dumped the mixture in, set the heat to medium and put a lid on the skillet. Just as a muffled sizzling sound started coming from the skillet, the two pieces of toast popped up. He took them out, smeared them with butter, and placed them on the plate. He checked the potatoes, which were beginning to soften and turn brown around the edges. He stirred them a bit with a spatula, and put the lid back on. He broke the two eggs into a small bowl, added salt, black pepper, and a quarter cup of milk, and beat the mixture until it was a nice even yellow color. He then took a small skillet from the cabinet, and put it on a burner turned on high. After a few seconds he took the stick of butter and swiped the skillet until it was coated in a nice sheen. Into this skillet, he poured the eggs and stirred slowly, flipping occasionally until he had a fluffy mound of scrambled eggs which he poured onto the plate next to the toast.

The potatoes were almost done, a medium brown color, so he pulled a sheet off the paper towel roll Lena kept next to the sink and spread it on a plastic plate. He laid two slices of bacon on the towel, pulled off another sheet and covered them with it. He set that plate in the microwave and set the timer for four minutes. As the microwave began humming, he turned his attention to the potatoes, stirring constantly until the potatoes were almost golden brown and the onion bits were dark brown with blackened edges. The smell of bacon, fried potatoes, and scrambled eggs filled the kitchen. Bradley's mouth started watering in anticipation of the meal that was to come.

He removed the bacon from the microwave, replacing it with a ceramic mug of water. He set the timer for two minutes and put the bacon and potatoes on the plate. When the microwave dinged, he took the mug of now hot water out and dumped in a teaspoon of Taster's Choice instant coffee.

He ate his breakfast at the tiny table with the view of the backyard, taking time to savor each bite, just the way Lena always nagged him to do. Funny, he thought, when she was around she always had to remind him to take his time and enjoy his food rather than bolting it down as if he had to eat quickly before someone took it away. Now that she was gone he found it easy to take his time eating.

"You were a great teacher, honey," he said. "I'm a better person because of you."

After finishing his meal, he took his time washing the dishes and other utensils and put everything back where it was supposed to be. He then wiped the table, countertop, and stove until they gleamed, and for good measure, swept the floor and took out the trash. Lena would have been proud.

Breakfast and morning cleaning chores done, he went back to their—his—bedroom, and took a duffle bag from the top shelf of the closet. He opened it and put it in the center of the bed.

He stood there for a while trying to decide what to pack.

The factor that would determine what went into the bag was—how long was he planning to be gone, and where in hell was he going—something he hadn't really thought about. It was just that, when he woke up that morning, he knew that he had to get out of this house, out of this town—away.

Far, far away. To a place where the thoughts that came unbidden wouldn't be so oppressive. To a place, perhaps, where the images in his mind would be associated with something pleasant.

Slowly, like the rising of leavened dough when the temperature is right, it came to him. He would go to the place he last remembered where his happiness for once almost matched hers. Three years ago, or maybe it was two, they'd decided to take a road trip during spring break, but to go someplace that neither of them had ever been before, and to a place that wasn't on the itinerary of the legions of students out of school for the period. The two of them had pored over a map of Virginia, Maryland, DC, Delaware, Pennsylvania, and New Jersey, one of the few paper maps still available for sale in a gas station. It has come down to the Amish country of Pennsylvania or somewhere along the Chesapeake Bay. In the end they'd simply flipped a coin—heads Chesapeake, tails Amish—and it had come up heads. Next, they'd looked at the map, from the north near Havre de Grace, Maryland, where the Susquehanna dumped its waters into the bay, south to Poconoke Sound, where on the east side of the bay, about five miles of peninsula in Virginia separated the bay from the Atlantic Ocean and on west the broad mouth of the Potomac flowed past innumerable small islands, joining the bay for its journey south to the Atlantic.

The town of Chesapeake Beach,

represented on the map by a black dot connected Maryland Route 4 by a single black line, caught their eye. Founded by the Washington and Chesapeake Bay Railway Company in 1894 as a resort for vacationers from the DC area, it was still a popular tourist destination, but hadn't come to the attention of students looking for a booze-fueled good time. The town only had one hotel, with a seafood restaurant next door, located close to the harbor and constructed in such a way that every room had a harbor view.

They hadn't known what to expect, and were surprised at the sedate pace of the place. It had a small water park that kept the families who'd brought children along occupied, a quiet beach backed by medium-high cliffs, a free railroad museum, and a surfing shop that offered lessons. Mostly, they'd wandered around taking pictures of each other and the turn of the century buildings that lined the narrow streets, or the fishing charter boats sailing into and out of the harbor, or in their hotel room making love or just spooning and enjoying each other's presence.

He remembered clearly how Lena had stood in the parking lot of the hotel on their last day, staring out at the bay, with the wind whipping her hair across her face.

"When we get old," she said. "We should move here. This would be the perfect place to spend eternity."

He hadn't answered her. Instead, he'd finished stowing the suitcase in the back of their 2010 Jeep Cherokee and held the passenger door for her to get in. Now, though, her words came back to him as if she'd just uttered them a few minutes ago—he could hear the soft, musical tone of her voice. And, he knew what he had to do.

He threw six pairs of pants, six shirts, six pairs of briefs, and six pairs of socks into the duffle. On top of that he put his toilet kit, an extra tube of toothpaste, his Canon digital camera and his Samsung laptop, along with two extra packages of batteries for the camera, the recharger for the computer, and a USB cable to allow uploading photos from the camera to the computer. He thought about including some reading material, but remembered that the hotel had a small shop in the lobby with a rack of paperbacks. The offerings when they visited had been a few *New York Times* bestsellers, romance novels, and thrillers. He would pass on the romance novels, which Lena devoured like popcorn, but figured they'd have the latest Robert Ludlum or James Patterson thriller that would take him through the two to three days he anticipated he'd be there.

Bag packed, he did a walk-through of the house, making sure the thermostats were set to minimize power consumption during his absence, the timers on the lights would turn them on at 6:00 pm and off at 6:00 am, not that that would fool a determined burglar, but it gave him a feeling of doing something positive, and besides, with his laptop in his possession, the only things left in the house worth anything were the TV set and DVR in the living room. He checked the refrigerator, which had a little milk and cheese, which he consumed. No sense, he reasoned, to return to a house full of the smell of spoiled milk and cheese. He made a mental reminder to swing by a grocery store on his way back.

After he was satisfied the house was in order, he took the bag out to the blue Jeep Cherokee sitting on the graveled driveway, and put it in the back seat.

Before setting out, he had one last task— no, strike that, two. First, he called Rebecca Davis's office. It was 8:45, and she'd already gone to her first lecture her teaching assistant said. Bradley gave the TA a message for her: 'Taking two weeks off. I'll be back in time for my students' final exams.' He then hit the red phone symbol on his cell phone and tapped the number '2' on the speed dial, Bill's number. After five rings, Bill's voice mail came on.

"You have reached the number of William Lewis. I'm unavailable at the moment, but if you'll leave your message and number after the tone, I promise I'll get back to you as soon as possible."

"Bill, this is Brad," Bradley said after the

phone beeped. "I'm taking off for about three days, going over to Chesapeake Bay. You remember that place Lena and I went to a couple years ago? I thought a few days there, remembering the good time we had, would help me clear my head. I'll call you as soon as I get there and check in to the hotel."

He put the phone in his shirt pocket, hopped up behind the wheel, turned on the engine, and was soon in Washington's ever-oppressive traffic, which for a few brief moments also helped take his mind off his grief.

CHAPTER 8

The traffic was chaotic and heavy through the District of Columbia and Maryland's Prince Georges County to the I-495 Beltway on-ramp near Greenbelt, and maddening from there to the off-ramp to Maryland Route 4 near Suitland. Once off the Beltway and through Upper Marlboro, where he stopped at a 7-Eleven to buy snacks and get a couple hundred dollars from an ATM, he headed south. Traffic southbound from Upper Marlboro petered out to just a few pickups, semis, and the occasional van. There was very little to see on the two-lane road, flanked at first by auto shops, antique stores, and roadside stands selling vegetables or curios, and then just trees, trees, the occasional open but unoccupied pasture, and then more trees.

At the start of his drive, the sky had been a deep blue, with just a smattering of cirrus clouds painted across the upper dome. But, thirty minutes past Upper Marlboro, the sky had turned light grey, and there was a mist in the air that caused distant objects to appear as fuzzy shapes. Then, the mist turned into a fog, a billowing white cloud that blocked Bradley's vision of everything more than ten feet in front of the Jeep. He didn't remember such spring weather conditions when he and Lena had driven this route before, but it had been unseasonably chilly, so he figured it was just a result of the extreme cold snap, the polar vortex, that had hit the area the past winter, dumping more snow in a month's time than they'd had in the past several years. March had been a cold, snowy month, and April wasn't looking to be any warmer, certainly not as warm as usual.

The featureless grey landscape drifting by outside the car windows had a hypnotic effect on him. He reached for the radio power button, but when he punched it to turn the radio on he was greeted by cracking static rather than the NPR station that he kept tuned in. He stabbed the 'scan' button, and listened as the tuner slid up and down the frequencies, encountering nothing but loud static on each. So much, he thought, for music to help him stay awake. He eased off on his speed, dropping to 40 mph, and began singing to himself. He didn't remember all the words to songs, and his voice had an irritating habit of sliding up and down octaves involuntarily, so that the only person who could stand listening to his singing, and then only in the shower, was himself. He sang the opening lines to songs, and then sang nonsense syllables or hummed the rest for the next twenty minutes until he got tired of hearing his off-key voice.

He began to consider that it might be prudent to pull off the highway and wait for the mist to clear, but without a radio to be able to listen to the weather report, he had no idea how long he might have to wait. On the other hand, in the thick mist, he risked rear-ending someone, or having a car coming from the opposite direction drift into his lane and hit him head-on. Mentally, he went through several potential accident scenarios, each gorier than the one before. He got himself so keyed up that by the time he'd finally decided that pulling off was the way to go, his hands were gripping the wheel so tightly his knuckles were turning white.

Just as he started pulling off his engine made a sputtering sound, then there was a loud 'pop,' and the engine stopped. It didn't wind down, or gradually stop. It just *stopped.* One second he could hear the hum of the Jeep's engine, and the next the only sound was the whisper of tires on the pavement, followed by the crunching sound as the right tires bit into the gravel of the shoulder. He coasted, steering gingerly, until the vehicle was completely off the pavement, then he turned the ignition key to 'off,' waited for a ten-count and turned it to 'start.' All that got him was a ticking sound. Then, he remembered that he had turned the headlights on when he first encountered the mist, so he turned them off, and tried the ignition again. Again, nothing but that irritating ticking.

With the engine off it didn't take long for the temperature in the car to drop. Bradley didn't know what the outside temperature was, but the prospect of shivering in an ice box of a car didn't appeal to him. He took his cell phone out of his pocket, hit Bill's speed dial number, and put the phone on speaker. All he got was a humming sound. He looked at the face. The signal indicator showed no bars, not even a hint of a signal.

No radio, no telephone, and an engine that wouldn't start, in the middle of nowhere in rural Maryland, in the fog, on a chilly day. Bradley catalogued all the things that had gone wrong in the space of a few hours. He sat there, drumming the heels of his hands on the steering wheel and cursing himself for ever coming up with the stupid idea to take a solitary road trip in the first place. He knew that eventually another vehicle would come along, but that left him with nothing to do but sit and wait. And, to add insult to injury, he'd neglected to stop at a 7-Eleven and buy snacks and drinks for the trip. Shit, he thought, with a dead engine and the poor visibility from the mist that had now closed in so tightly he could barely make out the edge of the Jeep's hood, reading was out of the question. Nor could he risk running down the charge on his laptop. Not that it would make a difference. If there was no radio or phone signal, he doubted there was a wireless network anywhere in the vicinity.

"Shit, shit, shit," he said as he beat the faux leather covered steering wheel.

A flickering of the mist, or in the mist, he couldn't be sure, caught his eye. Then the flickering, red and blue, came closer, coloring the mist around him as the flashes alternated.

For a moment, Bradley had the wild thought that an alien spaceship had landed and he was about to be abducted. His breath caught in his throat when he saw a dark, slender figure coming toward him through the mist. When the shadowy figure stopped near the driver's side window, he almost panicked, and he yelped when he heard a metallic tapping on the window.

Then, he heard, "Sir is everything okay?" His heartbeat, galloping like a thoroughbred in the final stretch, slowed a tiny bit. He let out a breath.

The figure pressed closer to the window, and through the mist, Bradley could make out the shiny badge on the left breast pocket of a brown shirt.

The cavalry had arrived.

CHAPTER 9

With a sense of relief Bradley lowered the window. Without the misty glass to obscure his vision, he could see the narrow face, thin-lipped smile and clear blue eyes of the man who had tapped on his window with the large flashlight he carried in his left hand. It did not go unnoticed that the man's right hand rested lightly on the butt of the revolver at his hip, but the gold badge reassured Bradley. He understood the officer's caution. A car stopped on the side of the road might be a stranded motorist, or in today's world, with so many guns in so many hands, it could also be something more deadly.

"Officer," he said. "Thank goodness you came along. My car won't start, and I can't get my phone to work."

The man relaxed. His hand was still near his weapon, but no longer on it.

"Can I see your license and registration, sir?" he asked.

"Sure thing." Bradley reached up to the passenger side visor, where he kept his registration certificate. He retrieved it and handed it out. "My driver's license is in my wallet. Do you mind if I get out so I can remove it?"

The officer stepped back, out of the arc of the door. "Sure, go ahead."

Bradley slowly opened the door, and, keeping his hands in plain sight, eased out of the vehicle. He turned to the left, so the officer could see clearly, and with his thumb and forefinger, extracted his wallet. He opened it, took the license from the plastic pocket and handed that over too. In several of the foster homes he'd been assigned to, he'd been warned from the age of twelve to always be careful and non-threatening when encountering the law. As one of his foster father's had said, "The po-leece, they scairt of a black man, don't matter his age. They jest soon shoot you as look at you, so don't you never give them no reason, boy, you understand." He never really understood until he was older and started reading news stories about young black men having fatal encounters with the forces of the law, often unarmed, but foolish enough to move too fast, talk to tough, or try to run away. This was the first time he'd ever been stopped, the first time, in fact, that he'd ever spoken to a law enforcement official. His heart still beat faster, but the man didn't look threatening, nor did he speak in the harsh tone Bradley had been told was the standard way cops spoke to black people.

The policeman looked at the license and registration, and, seemingly satisfied that everything was in order, handed them back.

"So, Mr. Matthews, you say your car won't start," he said. His tone *sounded* friendly enough, and he'd called Bradley *mister*, so maybe there was nothing to fear. "Did it happen all of a sudden, or had you been having troubles before?"

Good question, Bradley thought. He tried to remember. "It made a strange sound, kind of a whine, followed by a popping sound, and then just stopped."

"Okay, why don't you get in and try it again," the cop said. "Let me hear what it sounds like."

Bradley got back in and turned the key.

"Have you turned the key?" the cop asked. When Bradley nodded, he looked confused. "It didn't make a sound. I have never seen anything like this before. I think your engine is completely dead."

Well, Bradley thought, do you really think so? Of course it's dead. The question is what to do about it?

"What do you suggest I do about it?" Bradley asked.

"Well, you will not be driving it; that is for sure. I think you should allow me to give you a ride to Copper Cove and then you can have the town tow truck come here and tow it to the garage to be repaired."

Bradley hesitated. The guy was a cop, but he was also a stranger, regardless of his offer to be helpful. The man, who looked to be about two or three years older than Bradley, must have noticed his hesitance and figured out why. He said, "Oh, there is no reason to worry," he continued. "I am Jason Warfield, the sheriff of Copper Cove. There will be no charge for giving you a ride to town."

He seemed so sincere, Bradley felt his uneasiness abating. "Okay, Sheriff Warfield, if you don't mind."

Warfield smiled broadly. "It is not necessary to call me sheriff, Bradley; you do not mind if I call you Bradley, do you; you can just call me Jason."

"Good enough, Jason," Bradley said. "Let me get my duffle bag out of the back."

After retrieving his bag, locking the Jeep, and tossing the bag in the back seat of Warfield's car, Bradley sat in the front passenger seat. Warfield got behind the wheel.

"Please fasten your seatbelt," he said. "I cannot move the car until you do."

Bradley smiled as he clicked the seatbelt in place. Warfield, he thought, had a really funny way of talking, almost as if English wasn't his native language, or like a robot. And, his car interior was the neatest Bradley had ever seen. Most people will have at least a stray piece of paper or something on the back seat or floor, but Warfield's car looked— and smelled—like it had just come from the dealer's showroom.

Once he was buckled in, Warfield started the engine, and did a U-turn. He drove about fifty yards and then made a right turn onto a road Bradley didn't see, but could hear from the whooshing sound the cruiser's tires made, and the smoothness of the ride. Warfield looked straight ahead as he drove, not even checking the rearview mirror.

After a few minutes, Bradley found the silence unnerving.

"So, how far to, what did you call it, Copper Cove?" he asked.

"Approximately twelve to thirteen miles," Warfield said.

"How long have you been sheriff?"

"Uh . . . twenty years."

Bradley's mouth dropped open. Either the man was lying, had no concept of time, or was a hell of a lot older than he looked. He didn't look a day over forty, which would, if he told the truth, have made him twenty when he became sheriff. Bradley wasn't familiar with law enforcement recruiting guidelines or hiring policy, but that didn't sound right. And another thing, he thought, the way he talks doesn't sound right either.

"What did you do before you became sheriff?"

"Nothing," was the reply. Warfield's head

remained fixed, his eyes still on the road ahead.

Bradley began looking at the man as a challenge, much like he often had to do with shy freshmen at the start of a semester. The kind of kid who had potential, but who was intimidated by college and would sit in the back of the classroom hoping not to be noticed by the teacher—these were the students who caught Bradley's attention and evoked his desire to make a difference.

"You know," he said. "I've been along Route 4 before, and I don't recall ever seeing a sign for Copper Cove."

"That is because there is no sign."

"No sign? That's strange. Practically every other town . . . no, correction, every other town I've ever been through or passed by has a sign. Why would there be no sign for Copper Cove?"

Bradley noticed a tiny flicker of Warfield's eye that he could see, and a twitch of the muscle below that eye.

"I do not know why there is no sign," Warfield said in that toneless, robotic voice that was beginning to grate on Bradley's nerves. "We have a small population, only 200 people. No one comes to visit, and the people who live in Copper Cove do not have any desire to visit other places. So, I presume it has never been found necessary to have a sign."

That was Warfield's longest speech since

he tapped on Bradley's car window, and it was as uninformative as his clipped sentences had been. It was as if the man had a programmed set of responses, reminding Bradley of the movie, 'The Stepford Wives,' and the robotic women in it. *Get a grip, Bradley, it's just the dreary weather and the car breaking down on a deserted road getting to you.*

"So, you mean the residents of your town never go anywhere?"

"Some do, most do not."

"What do you people do for entertainment, just sit around watching TV?"

Warfield didn't respond. He just continued to drive, his hands at two and ten on the steering wheel, his eyes looking straight ahead, as if he hadn't heard the question.

Just as Bradley was about to ask another probing question, they emerged from the mist.

It wasn't a gradual diminution of mist that he would have expected. One second everything outside the car was a wavering, misty grey; the next, the air was clear, the sky above was bright blue, and the sun was shining, casting stark shadows of the trees alongside the highway, a straight, two-lane ribbon of blue-grey with a solid yellow line down the middle that sliced ahead through the verdant green countryside like an arrow.

"Wow," Bradley said. "The fog cleared up awful fast."

Warfield pointed to the inside rearview mirror. "Still pretty thick behind us. We almost always have good weather in Copper Cover, though."

Bradley craned around and looked through the rear window. Behind the cruiser he saw a wall of grey. He was sure his eyes must be playing tricks on him, though, because it looked less like a billowing cloud than a grey wall. He could only see up so far, but it looked it rose up several hundred feet in the air, and the front edge looked like it had billowed up against a glass wall set across the highway. He turned back in his seat, shaking his head. It had to be some kind of optical illusion. Fog didn't act that way. He shook his head. This, he thought, was shaping up to be one strange day.

Their entry into Copper Cove was as abrupt as their exit from the mist had been. The stately trees on both side of the highway gave way to several red brick homes with wide front porches and neatly trimmed lawns and detached wooden garages, which gave away in turn to a simple, two-lane street lined by small one and two-story buildings, shops and stores typical of small, rural Maryland towns, a barbershop, an antique store, a small combination grocery-drug-hardware store, and a bed and breakfast with old English lettering in the sign identifying it as the *Copper Cove Inn*. The sidewalks along the main street, the only street, were elevated two feet above the street surface, with steps cut into them at every other building.

It didn't take long to get from the north end to the south end of town, and that was, in fact, pretty much the end of town. A gas station and garage sat on the left side of the street, and a two story building with a faded sign over the front door that said, *CITY HALL/SHERIFF'S OFFICE.* Bradley expected Warfield to turn in and park there. Instead, the lawman turned left and parked his cruiser in front of the garage. Bradley looked at him with raised brows.

"Oh, I am stopping here so that you can make arrangements for Philo to go out to the highway and tow your car," Warfield said.

"Of course," Bradley said. "I knew that."

They went inside where Philo, a six-three beanpole of a man with an acne-scarred complexion and unkempt red hair that stuck out in all directions except where it was plastered down by black grease, took Bradley's keys and told him he'd go out and tow his car in right after noon.

"You couldn't possibly do it earlier?" Bradley asked. He looked around. Philo didn't seem to be doing anything, and there were no other customers.

"Sorry, but I done promised Mayor Bryant I'd come over to fix his office air conditioner," Philo said. "The mayor, he don't like to be kept waitin', ain't that right, sheriff?"

"If you say so, Philo," Warfield said. He

turned to Bradley. "If it makes you feel any better, it is unlikely anyone will steal your vehicle, but I will take you to Eve Stark's inn where you can rest and get some food, and I will go back and keep a watch on it for you."

"That's really nice of you, sheriff," Bradley said. "But, I really can't ask you to do that."

"It is no problem, Bradley, and please call me Jason. Now, if you will give Philo your vehicle key, I will take you to Eve's."

Without waiting for Bradley to answer, Warfield spun on his heels and left the garage.

CHAPTER 10

"I am Eve Stark, the proprietor of this inn," the striking, dark-haired, blue-eyed woman said. "But, you may call me Eve."

She spoke in the same monotone as Warfield, but somehow, on her it seemed alluring to Bradley rather than weird as it did with the sheriff.

"Thank you, Eve," he said. "I'm Bradley Matthews, but my friends call me Bradley or Brad."

"Which would you prefer?" She cocked her head to one side, causing a lock of raven hair to fall over a sky-colored eye.

"It's . . . entirely up to you." Bradley found himself almost tongue tied, reminding him of how he'd been before meeting Lena. Before her, he'd been unable to talk in complete sentences to any pretty girl. "I g-guess you can call me Brad if you'd like, or Bradley if that's more comfortable."

"Very well, Bradley," she said. "Welcome to Copper Cove and to the Copper Cove Inn. I would imagine that you have not eaten since breakfast, so please put your bag here by the desk and have a seat in the dining room. I will have lunch prepared shortly."

She ushered him into the small dining room just off the even tinier lobby and showed him to a table near the back corner where he had a great view of an otherwise empty room with five other tables. He looked for a menu.

"May I see the menu?" he asked.

"We do not have a menu," she replied. "The cook prepares a different meal each day. I believe that lunch today is beef stew and home fried potatoes. I assure you, you will like it. Would you like coffee or tea before you are served your food?"

Strange custom, sort of like some of the older Italian restaurants in Baltimore and DC, not at all what he would have expected, but it was a small town, and Bradley's experience with small towns was exactly nil, so he just nodded, and said, "Coffee sounds good, and so does the stew. Say, you wouldn't happen to have today's *Washington Post* by any chance?"

She was turning away, but turned back at his question.

"*Washington Post* . . . oh, you mean the newspaper. No, I'm sorry, but we do not have any newspapers here."

Now, that was stranger still. He couldn't remember going anywhere that didn't have at least *USA Today* with its colorful headlines and pictures. Then, he looked around the empty room and noticed what else was missing—a wall-mounted TV with *Fox News* blaring out its hype, or *ESPN* with endless sports. Oh well, he thought, a few hours until that guy . . . Philo . . . got the Jeep running, and he'd be on his way. Hopefully the food would at least be palatable.

"That's okay," he said. "Do you have Wi-Fi, so I can check the news on my laptop?"

"Why fie?" She looked confused.

Damn, no newspapers, no TV, and she doesn't even know what a wireless computer network is. *I've heard of one-horse towns, but this takes the cake.* "No, not *why fie*," he said. "Wi-Fi. It's a computer network that allows you to connect to the Internet without having to use a cable."

She smiled. Rustic or not, she had a beautiful smile. "No, I am afraid we do not have a . . . computer connection here."

Shit. Guess I'll have to try to connect with my Smart Phone. I hate like hell having to try and read that small screen.

He took his phone from his pocket and swiped the screen to activate it. When he tried getting a connection by tapping the globe icon nothing happened. Then he looked closer and saw that the connection icon was almost transparent and didn't show any bars—not a single one. No wireless phone connection. *Where am I? Is this some kind of communications black hole?* "I don't seem to be able to get a phone signal in here," he said. "Where's the best place to get one?"

Stark walked back to the table and stood behind him, looking over his shoulder.

"That is a telephone, right? Is it also wireless like your . . . computer? I am afraid we do not have wireless telephone signals here."

Bradley breathed out noisily. "Is there someplace else in town I can get a signal?"

"No," Stark said. "When I said that we do not have signals here, I meant that we do not have them anywhere in Copper Cove. Why do you wish to use your telephone?"

"Oh, I just want to check the news."

Her eyes widened slightly and she looked confused. "You use your telephone to check the news? That is very interesting. But, I am afraid it will not be possible. Now, if you will excuse me, I will see to your meal."

Bradley watched her walk away, watched until the door to what he assumed was the inn's kitchen closed and cut off his view. For the briefest of moments he was distracted by the sway of her hips beneath the mid-thigh length skirt she wore. But, after she was gone his mind went back to the oddities of Copper Cove.

For one thing, except for Philo, who talked like a dozen other small town people he'd encountered over the years, Eve Stark and Jason Warfield sounded like characters from a Victorian drama. They were the first real live people he'd ever met who spoke without using contractions. He replayed his conversations with them in his mind, and realized that neither of them had used a contraction even once. He then remembered that Warfield's squad car hadn't had a radio, nor had he seen a radio, telephone, or TV in Philo's place. It was like he'd been transported back to the eighteenth century or earlier.

He'd heard of small towns around the country whose people limited use of technology. Until now, he'd thought it was just an urban legend, but apparently, his Jeep had picked just such a place in which to break down. The last place he'd expected to find such a community was in the state of Maryland, and, within spitting distance of the nation's capital. Admittedly he knew very little about the state, or the region for that matter. He'd heard of a county in the western part of the state that was ultra-conservative, and had even tried to secede and become an independent state, but it was way off the beaten path, not on a main highway linking the urban areas like Baltimore and DC to the tourist mecca of the Chesapeake Bay. Some of the smaller communities along the Chesapeake were also supposedly traditional and conservative, but with the number of vacationers from Washington, Baltimore, and other eastern seaboard cities visiting the bay area so frequently, it didn't seem likely that this area would have such a place, or so he'd thought before now. He would have given anything to be able to boot up his laptop or Smart Phone and Google Copper Cove to see what the Internet had about the place.

When your normal diversions are unavailable, the mind has a tendency to wander down strange paths, and that's what was happening to Bradley now. *What the hell kind of place have I ended up in?* If a buck toothed, tow head with a fiddle appeared he would have panicked. When the door through which Eve Stark had vanished swung open he did jump back in his chair.

But, there was no kid with a straw in his mouth cradling a beaten up fiddle, it was just Stark balancing a large silver tray on which sat a plate and a bowl which she placed on the table opposite him. The dishes looked like museum pieces, sturdy early American crockery with crudely painted blue scenes of trees and mountains baked into the surface.

She put a large bowl of beef stew in front of him. Next came a large plate containing a large pile of golden brown home fried potatoes, two squares of cornbread, and a pile of green beans, which she put beside the bowl. She then arranged a spoon, fork and knife around the containers, and took a white linen napkin off the tray and handed it to him. He took in a deep breath. The smells set his mouth to watering, and reminded him that he hadn't eaten since breakfast.

Stark waited until he'd placed the napkin on his lap and picked up the spoon, preparing to dip it into the stew.

"I hope you enjoy your meal," she said. Then, she turned and walked away.

He watched her go, again his eyes drawn to the way her hips swayed beneath the long skirt. He slapped his left wrist with his right hand. "Stop it, Brad," he growled under his breath. "You shouldn't be ogling another woman so soon after . . . well, anyway, she's probably married, and her husband might not approve."

She'd invited him to enjoy the food, and the aromas wafting up from the table were tempting, so he dug in.

Charles Ray

CHAPTER 11

And, enjoy it he did, enjoyed it more in fact than he'd enjoyed a meal in a long time. The beef stew was thick and rich and had a slight tang of oregano, the home fries had been liberally sprinkled with garlic powder before being fried, and the green beans had a taste of onion and pepper. The cornbread was sweet, with kernels of sweet corn mixed in, and Stark had brought him a pitcher of iced tea and a large 12-ounce glass. He asked for seconds on the beef stew and cornbread and finished the entire pitcher of tea, and sat back massaging his stomach, thoughts of how strange Copper Cove held at bay for the moment.

He still had the dining room to himself. Stark had gone back to the front desk, although to do what Bradley didn't know, because she didn't seem to have any other guests, but he didn't think it would have been polite to inquire.

Just as he was about to drift off to sleep from the combined effects of the heavy meal and the quiet of the room, Philo came striding in, his big brogans making slapping sounds on the hardwood floor.

"There you be, Mr. Matthews," he boomed from across the room. "Figured I'd find you here. How was your lunch?"

Bradley blinked to clear his vision. "Uh, hello, Philo. Thanks, it was great food. When will my car be ready?"

Philo, who had stopped at the edge of the table across from Bradley, frowned and scratched at his right ear.

"Well now, that's kinda the problem see," he said. "The starter motor on your car done blown completely. I gotta replace it."

"Will that take long?"

"Uh, installin' it might take me three or four hours . . . but, the problem is, I ain't got one in stock. I gotta order it, and it's gonna take a week, mebbe ten days for it to get here."

Bradley stiffened, his hands gripping the edge of the table so hard he created arrow-shaped furrows in the linen tablecloth. "Ten days! I can't sit around here that long."

"I can put you up in a room here," Eve Stark said. Bradley hadn't even heard her enter. She moved up beside Philo. "The place, as you have no doubt noticed, is not exactly crowded, and I think a few days here, without the distractions of the city might be just what

76

you need right now."

Her gaze held him transfixed as she spoke. Bradley felt that she'd bored directly into his brain. Her expression was sympathetic, almost mournful, as if she understood what he was going through.

"I really don't want to be a bother," he said. "I . . . think I should be getting back to the city."

Her expression tightened, and Bradley saw a quick flash of emotion in her dark eyes, then she smiled. "Come now, Mr. Matthews . . . Bradley." She paused, looking quizzically at him as if expecting him to say something. When he didn't speak, she continued, "You and I both know that the last place you want to be at this moment is back in the city where so many sad thoughts haunt you."

He felt a chill stab through his chest. "How . . . how do you know I have sad thoughts? Are you come kind of fortune teller?"

She smiled more broadly. "No, Bradley, I am not a fortune teller. The sadness is apparent on your face. I would hazard a guess that you have suffered a great loss, and you were getting away from the city to cope with that loss."

She might deny being a fortune teller, but she'd hit so close to the truth, Bradley wasn't convinced she wasn't some kind of shaman; or maybe a supremely gifted confidence woman. Her gaze, as soft as it was, bored right through him. But, he thought, he wasn't carrying much cash, and she was right, he did need to get away from the city, and the place was quiet and out of the way. *What have I got to lose? A few days here in Mayberry just might help me get my mind settled. I can drive on to the bay after I decompress.*

"W-well, you're sort of right," he said. "But, this isn't exactly the place I had in mind to get away to."

"Bradley, this is precisely the place you need to be." He opened his mouth, but she shut him up with a wave of her hand. "No, please, hear me out. You were no doubt planning to go to some resort near the bay?" He nodded. She was pretty good. Then again, the highway connected to routes to the bay, so it would be easy to guess. He gave her a skeptical look. "Again, I am no fortune teller, but the road you were on does lead to Chesapeake Bay, so it stands to reason that it was your destination. Now, at such a place there will be many other tourists. What you need is a place where you can be alone with your thoughts . . . where you can deal with your loss without distraction."

He had to acknowledge the sense in what she said. And, she didn't sound like a scam artist; just a concerned small town dweller with good insights. "Okay, I suppose you're right. So, what are your nightly rates?"

Her head slowly went up and down, and a smile of satisfaction lit up her face.

"I think you will find the rates for a room with meal here most reasonable, Bradley Matthews. For ten days, you will pay me . . . one hundred dollars."

His mouth and eyes opened round together and he stared for a few seconds at her. Finally, he gulped and spoke, "You're kidding. You said you have no other guests . . . how can you let me stay for such a low rate?"

"The inn is empty. If you do not stay, I will make nothing. If you stay, I will make one hundred dollars. Does that not sound like a situation that benefits both of us? What I ask in return for your most reasonable room and board rate is that you tell me stories of life outside."

"Life outside . . . outside what?"

"Why, life outside Copper Cove of course."

Charles Ray

CHAPTER 12

When Eve said she wanted Bradley to tell her stories of life outside Copper Cove, he had thought she was joking. He quickly learned that her request had been literal. It wasn't just computers she didn't understand.

After a frustrating hour of trying to explain wireless networks and the cloud to her—in truth, he didn't really understand them all that well himself, but in the kingdom of the blind the one-eyed man is king, so she hung on his every word, stopping him every few sentences to have him explain something—he was ready to throw his hands up in disgust. He was coming to the conclusion that he was, in fact, a lousy teacher.

"You're harder to teach than a member of the Tea Party," he said.

"What does attending a tea party have to do with learning?" she asked.

"What, you've never heard of the Tea Party?"

She blinked and looked at him. "Of course I have heard of the tea party," she said. "There was the famous Boston Tea Party, when the colonials destroyed British cargos of tea in protest over taxes imposed by the crown, and there was the tea party in the book written by Lewis Carroll—"

"No, not those tea parties," Bradley objected. "Although, the people who started it often like to talk about the Boston Tea Party as a model for their movement." He then went on to explain the political phenomenon that came to be known as the Tea Party Movement, and how it got its start in the mid-1980s when two super rich ultra-conservative brothers with ties to the chemical industry founded an organization, along with financial support from many major corporations, designed to revive the paleoconservative movement that grew up in opposition to Franklin D. Roosevelt's New Deal expansion of government in the 30s and 40s. Strongly anti-communist and anti-globalization, and opposed to the stimulus packages of the Bush *and* Obama administrations, it took on the name Tea Party, and became closely associated with the ultra-conservative element of the Republican Party. Somewhat isolationist, regarding foreign policy, they nonetheless support pre-emptive military action in cases where they feel core values are threatened—often without specifically defining those values. He then explained that these are people who want to turn back the clock to a perceived 'golden' past, and refuse to believe any fact that doesn't fit their preconceived beliefs.

When he stopped speaking, she regarded him intently. Finally, she said, "I think I see the point you are trying to make, and I agree with you that people who think like that are mistaken. While there were many things in the past that are worthy of preserving, there were just as many that should never have been—slavery for instance. I think I should be insulted that you would compare me with such people."

"No, please," Bradley said. "I didn't mean to compare you with these wingnuts, and I certainly didn't mean to insult you. Please forgive my slip of the tongue. It's just that there are so many things that people take for granted that you seem to be totally unaware of. I find that strange."

They'd been sitting side by side in a wooden porch swing on the back verandah of the inn. Despite the space between them, Bradley was uncomfortably aware of the heat from her body. When she reached across the space and laid a hand on his arm, he felt a tingle.

"I do not think you intended an insult," she said softly. "And, I am not offended by what you said." She smiled. "You are correct. There are many things about the world outside Copper Cove that I do not know. I do not travel much . . . in fact, I have never really traveled at all. My duties here keep me too busy for me to pay much attention to affairs outside the town. Until you came, I suppose I had never had the occasion to think about such things, and I find them fascinating. And, I might add, you have a wonderful way of telling them."

"It's too bad there's no Internet connection. With that I'd be able to show you things you could never imagine."

She withdrew her hand and laid a forefinger against her cheek. "Perhaps, but I find listening to you quite pleasant, far more pleasant I think, than merely reading about things on this Internet of yours."

His cheeks felt warm. In truth, he'd found it pleasant to talk to her. Sitting here next to this beautiful, enigmatic woman, her expression guileless, and her apparent lack of knowledge of the world outside her town refreshing to someone who had spent his three decades dealing with people with agendas—Lena and Bill excepted—and, for a moment, he'd forgotten about the heavy weight of sadness that had borne down upon him since Lena's death.

"Thank you," he said. "I find it pleasant to talk to you too."

Was he flirting? So soon after Lena's death, would it even be appropriate? Or, was this just his reaction to a warm and welcoming, and totally naïve personality? He couldn't deny that Eve Stark was an attractive woman. Despite the slightly old-fashioned clothing she wore, longer than normal skirts and long-sleeved blouses, he could not help but notice that she had a nice body. Long shapely legs, small, but finely turned hips, and conical breasts that strained against the fabric of her blouse caught his attention whenever she was in sight. Her eyes, devoid of makeup, seemed to draw him into their depths. Her lips, only slightly tinted with a pinkish red color which didn't really look like lip stick, or even the lip gloss that was all the rage with some women, were full and luscious, and when she smiled, dimples formed on both cheeks. She was, without doubt, what his friend Bill would call 'one hot number.' And, to add to the heat building in his chest and loins, she seemed to be genuinely interested in him. Lena had been the first woman to ever show any real interest in him. He'd had a few of his female students feign interest in their pursuit of better grades, or in a couple of cases, a passing grade, but nothing like this. It was baffling, but pleasant.

Placing a hand on his shoulder, Stark stood. "Since it will take such a long time for Philo to repair your vehicle, we will have many opportunities to talk. I think, though, that you should get some rest now. I will see you at breakfast in the morning."

She turned and walked away. Bradley sat

alone in the swing for several minutes after she'd gone, thinking that being stuck in Copper Cove might not be such a bad idea after all.

CHAPTER 13

Upon leaving Bradley in the dining room, Eve Stark retired to her room on the top floor of the inn. She flipped the light switch as she entered, casting the small bedroom in an orange light from the small lamp on the table beside the large four-poster bed.

Kicking off her shoes, she went to a low table in the far corner and knelt before it. On the table was a mirror in a brass frame, a rectangular shape, two feet wide and four feet hide propped against the wall. It looked too large for the table. In front of the mirror was a brass candle holder with a black candle. She opened a drawer in the table and withdrew a box of wooden matches. Taking a match, she struck it on the side of the box, and lit the candle.

The candle flame flickered in a slight breeze that wafted through the room. The smell of candlewax and some sweet, undefinable fragrance filled the room.

She reached into the drawer again, and withdrew a black lace cloth, which she draped over her head, completely covering her hair. Then, she bowed low, her gaze fixed on the candle's wavering flame.

"Oh, master, your unworthy servant appears before you," she intoned in a voice that sounded deep and guttural, not at all the tone she'd used when speaking with the new—only—guest of the inn.

Silence greeted her, deep, oppressive silence that would have unsettled a normal person. But, Eve Stark was not a *normal* person. She was the emissary. The conduit between the master and the world of mortals, she was not *immortal*, not in the sense of living forever, but neither was she truly mortal. She was just . . . what she was, and had been for so long, she'd stopped thinking about it.

Until the arrival of Bradley Matthews, the young man with the dark face and brooding expression who, despite the great weight of sorrow he bore, had the time to sit and talk with her as if she was a normal person, she had never considered her condition. Now, her mind was a maelstrom of conflicting thoughts, thoughts she hoped would not be apparent to the one she waited for.

The candle flame flickered again, only this time it was not a stray breeze that caused the movement. She felt the presence even before the glass of the mirror began undulating in time with the flickering of the flame. The mirror glass began to turn a milky color, obscuring her reflection.

The voice seemed to be coming from every point in the room, dark and sepulchral, it still, after all the years, sent chills through her body, *"I am here my child. I see that the chosen one has arrived? Does he meet with your approval?"*

"Yes, Master Ahnok," she replied. "He came just as you predicted, and I do approve of him. He is unlike the other men of this place."

"Very good. Now, you must convince him to stay so that he might fulfill his destiny."

"But, master, why can you not simply command him to stay?"

A wave of icy cold air swept through the room causing her to shiver, from fear as much as from the temperature.

"Do not question me, young one!" The voice thundered in her ears.

"I . . . I meant no offense, master," she said. "I only thought that you could merely command him to stay. Please forgive my impertinence."

"I forgive you, my child. I know you meant no disrespect. I will explain; in order for the prophecy to be fulfilled, it is necessary that the chosen one come of his own free will. It is your mission to see that he makes the right choice. Do I make myself clear?"

"Most clear, master. I will not fail you."

"See that you do not. I have waited long, too long. The last one was a failure. We cannot fail with this one."

The voice faded away and the mirror's surface once again became still. The temperature in the room came back to normal. But, Eve Stark still felt immensely cold, and she couldn't stop shivering.

CHAPTER 14

After a light supper and his time with Eve Stark, Bradley retired to his room, his mind swirling with images of her and fragments of their disjointed and somewhat surreal conversation. He washed in the small bathroom, put on his pajamas and sat up in bed for an hour, trying to read one of the mystery novels he'd packed, but had been unable to focus on the words, so he finally gave up, turned off the light and burrowed under the light blanket.

For the first time since the doctor had informed them of Lena's cancer, he fell into a deep, untroubled slumber. The dreams, though, began the instant he fell asleep.

He was in a place he did not recognize, surrounded by a billowing grey-white haze so thick he could not see his feet. He stood upon a spongy surface. The haze, mist, fog, he didn't know what to call it, closed in around him. There was no sound, not even the rush of air entering and leaving his nostrils. It was an ominous quiet. He wasn't sure how he knew this was a mystery, but he knew.

Moving forward over the spongy surface was easy, but he hesitated because he couldn't see where he was going. Looking back over his shoulder, he couldn't see where he'd come from. Hell, he couldn't tell where he was. It was just a cocoon of formless grey, reminding him of the fog he and Warfield had driven through on the way to Copper Cove.

Yes, he thought, that's where I'm coming from—Copper Cove. What a strange town. He stopped walking as he thought about it. The funny way Eve—he found himself easily calling her by her first name—and Warfield spoke, her lack of familiarity with things that most people took for granted . . . and, now that his mind was on the issue, the fact that he'd seen no other people in the town; no one walking the sidewalks, no other cars. He assumed that the inn must have a cook, but he'd only seen three people in town. Strange, very strange, he thought. Like Alice, I've falling down the rabbit hole. Next, I guess I'll see the White Rabbit or the Mad Hatter.

He started walking again. The mist seemed to be thinning out, but he still saw nothing but grey. The difference now, though, was he thought he heard something, a faint sound at the very limits of his hearing. He focused carefully on the sound and moved, hopefully, for it.

He had no idea how long he'd been

walking. Time had no meaning in this place without referent points. But, the sound was getting clearer if not louder. It sounded like a voice, a woman's voice, and as he walked he realized that he recognized the voice. It was Eve.

"Bradley, come to me," the disembodied voice said. *"Come to me."*

The tone was . . . he found it hard to describe, like one of those vampish women in old black and white movies from the 40s and 50s, seductive and come hither. Not at all the way Eve seemed in real life.

He kept walking. The mist kept getting thinner. Then, up ahead, he saw a shape. At first, a vaguely human shape, which slowly solidified into the pleasantly curved shape of a woman, and then when he was about ten feet away, the facial features were visible, and the face he saw belonged to Eve Stark. But, it was the rest of her that caused his mouth to drop open. A sheer cloth was draped over one shoulder, leaving one conical breast bare, flowing down across a fat belly, covering both shapely legs, stopping at the top of her naked feet. The rest of her, if the dark triangle below her belly was any indication, was just as naked.

Bradley found himself becoming aroused; aroused in a way he hadn't been since the last time he was with Lena just before the doctor delivered her cancer diagnosis. For a heartbeat he felt guilty that the sight of another woman, even in a dream, could create such feelings, then he reminded himself that it was only a dream. Dreams didn't count. He continued forward until she was just beyond the reach of his outstretched arms. He stopped and stared at her.

"*I want you, Bradley. I must have you.*"

"This is a dream, babe," he said. "So, have at me." *Where the hell did that come from? I've never talked like that in my life.*

"*Are you sure, Bradley? I need you, but—*"

"But, what? Hey, it's just a dream, so there should be no problem."

"*It is not a dream. Once we are together, it is forever.*"

He'd been reaching for her, but that brought him up short. "W-what do you mean, it's no dream? Of course it's a dream."

She reached out toward him. Something, he wasn't sure what, caused him to take a step backwards.

"*Why do you move away from me? Do you not find me desirable?*"

Good question. In the flesh, he *had* noticed her, the sway of her hips and the curve of her breasts, and here in his dream, with nothing between them but a semi-transparent piece of cloth, he had to admit that she was a hot woman. But, something, a nagging itch in the back of his mind, was causing him to hesitate. Then, he looked closely into her eyes, and felt a chill. Her eyes were not just dark, they were a deep obsidian, so inky black they seemed to absorb rather than reflect light, and there wasn't a trace of white, just two black orbs filling her eye sockets.

He staggered back further, raising his hands. "W-what the hell! You're not Eve. What the hell are you?" His throat felt tight and his mouth dry. He could feel his heart beating against his ribs.

"*I am Eve,*" the thing in front of him said. "*And, I am for you, Bradley Matthews.*"

"No, you stay the hell away from me." He spun on his heels and started running.

The apparition that appeared to be Eve Stark did not go after him. She, it, stood looking sadly after him.

"*You will return, Bradley Matthews,*" she said. "*You will be mine. You are fated to be mine!*"

Back in his room, Bradley shot straight up in bed, tossing the covers aside. His breath came in ragged gasps, and his heart felt as if it would punch through his chest wall. His skin was wet and clammy with sweat. *Damn,* he thought, *I must have been having a doozy of a nightmare.* He struggled to remember what it was that had scared him awake, but nothing came. *I wonder why I don't remember?*

Charles Ray

CHAPTER 15

At first, William Lewis could only sit speechless and stare at her. He'd seen her before, of course, but never this close up and never sitting in such a manner that her hiked up skirt showed such an amazingly beautiful expanse of flesh.

But, he was here on important business. Friday was also one of the busiest days at the lobbying firm where he worked, as everyone prepared for the weekend. While most Washington, DC workers looked at the weekend as a time to relax with family, and hope no crisis broke out to yank them back to their offices, the lobbying industry does a lot of its work on weekends. Golfing outings, sailing, and quiet trips to hunting cabins in the West Virginia mountains, these were among the lobbyists' stock and trade. It was his job to prepare dossiers on potential 'clients,' to give the lobbyist assigned the case an idea of what approach would be most effective. Stacks of folders awaited on his desk in his K Street office.

He cleared his throat, "Uh, thank you for seeing me on such short notice, Professor Davis," he said. It was half past eight. He knew from Bradley that this was before her first classes.

"On the phone you said it was about Bradley Matthews, and that it was urgent." She tugged at the hem of her skirt, only reducing the exposed thigh by a few millimeters.

"Yeah, I got this voice message from him yesterday, but when I tried calling him back I got an out of service message."

"Maybe he was just in a place without service," she said. "He left a message with my secretary, saying he was going to some little town on the Chesapeake."

"That's what he told me, but I know the town he's going to, and it has cell service. I tried him again just before coming here to see you, and still couldn't reach him."

Her watched as she leaned forward, the neck of her blouse ballooning out, revealing the rounded swell of her breasts. Any other time he would have enjoyed the view, but now he was worried about his friend.

"It's not like him not to stay in touch," he continued.

"Why come to me?"

He shook his head and ran his hand through his hair.

"I don't know. I suppose . . . well, there's

no one else since Lena . . ."

"I know," she said. "I believe he mentioned to me once that the three of you were a close-knit group." Her brow knitted. "You *are* worried. If you think he's in trouble, why don't you call the police?"

He shook his head again. "Believe me, I thought about that, but who would I call?"

"I don't know, how about the police in the town he's going to? Maybe you should call them?"

His cheeks reddened. "Oh, yeah, I guess I wasn't thinking straight." He looked at the phone on her desk. "Uh, you mind if I use your phone? I need to call directory assistance."

"Of course." She pushed the phone across the desk toward him.

Unaccustomed to using anything but a cell phone, it took him several tries to get directory assistance, and then a few more fumbling minutes to remember the name of the town Bradley had been planning to visit—Chesapeake Beach. There followed more waiting while directory assistance looked for the number of the police department responsible for the town, which turned out to be the Calvert County Sheriff's Office in Prince Frederick, a town about 30 miles south of Chesapeake Beach. He got through to a deputy sheriff, gave him Bradley's name and description and asked if he could check to see if he was currently in Chesapeake

Beach. The deputy informed him that he would dispatch a car to the town to check and would call him back.

He put his hand over the mouthpiece. "You mind if I give him this number and wait here for the call?"

"Not at all," Davis said. "You have me worried now."

He gave the deputy the number and hung up.

After a few moments of strained silence, Davis leaned forward again, placing her elbow on the desk. "So, while we wait, why don't you tell me about your relationship with Brad?"

Talking to other people about the bonds that had developed among the three of them—and he still thought of them as a threesome—was something he'd never done, and was pretty sure that neither Bradley nor Lena had either. But, this strikingly beautiful older woman, who he was now beginning to really notice, made it comfortable. He found himself describing how the three of them had met as freshmen, bonded, and become inseparable. He was describing how Lena's death had devastated them, especially Bradley, when the phone rang. Davis answered, listened for a few seconds, and passed the phone to him.

"It's the sheriff from Calvert County," she said.

"William Lewis," he said when he took the

phone.

"Mr. Lewis, this is Sheriff Baxter from Calvert County," the nasal voice on the other end said. "You spoke with one of my deputies a little while ago about a friend of yours who's supposed to be in Chesapeake Beach, a Bradley Matthews?"

"Yes, sheriff, I did. Did you find him? Is he okay?"

There was a pause.

"Well, Mr. Lewis, I don't rightly know how to say this. We checked the hotels in and around the town . . . your friend didn't check into any of them. You sure that's where he was headed?"

William's stomach felt like he'd swallowed a ball of lead. "Uh, that's where he said he was going," he said.

"Maybe he changed his mind and went somewhere else," Baxter said. "Check Ocean City, or he might've even decided to go down south to Virginia."

If it had been anyone else, he might have thought that, but this was Bradley. The man *never* changed his plans. Of the three, Bradley had been the anal retentive, stick-to-the-schedule one whenever William and Lena wanted to do something impromptu. Something was wrong. But, he wasn't sure what he should do about it.

"Thanks, sheriff," he said. "I'll do that."

He gave the sheriff his cell number just in case he learned anything new, and hung up.

"So," Rebecca Davis said. "What will you do now?"

He shrugged. "I wish I knew."

"You'll let me know if you hear anything."

He'd picked up on the worry in her voice.

"Of course," he said. "If I hear anything, you'll be the first person I call." Actually, despite his worry about his friend, he was thinking that Rebecca Davis was a hot looking woman, despite probably being ten or fifteen years older than him, and he'd find an excuse to call her whether he heard anything from Bradley or not.

CHAPTER 16

After showering, Bradley pulled on a pair of jeans and a long-sleeved polo shirt and went down to have breakfast. Eve was standing at the entrance to the dining room. As he approached her, he smiled, but was taken aback when she averted her gaze. But, she quickly recovered and smiled weakly back at him.

"Good morning, Mr. Matthews," she said. "I trust you slept well."

He didn't pick up right away that she'd changed from addressing him by his first name, or that her demeanor wasn't as warm as it had been the evening before.

"Actually, I didn't," he said. "I had this really weird nightmare or something."

She'd been turning to pick up a coffee urn on a table behind her. Her hand stopped in mid-air, and she looked back at him.

"A . . . dream . . . what was it about?"

"Well, that's just it . . . I know I dreamed about something disturbing, but I don't remember what it was. It's really strange, because I usually remember my dreams."

She let out the breath she'd been holding.

"T-that *is* strange. What would you like for breakfast this morning?"

He could not help but smile. The way she'd changed the subject was masterful. It put him at ease. *Maybe staying here a few days might not be a bad idea.*

"You mean I get a choice this morning? Yesterday, it was, eat whatever the cook prepares."

She returned his smile. "For you, the cook is prepared to do whatever you wish."

"Okay, I'll have scrambled eggs, toast, hashed browns, coffee, and tomato juice," he said. "Will that be possible?"

"Of course, Mr. Matthews, for you anything is possible."

"Why all the sudden formality? Last night we were Bradley and Eve."

"I . . . I was not sure you would remember . . . or want me to—"

He placed his hand on hers, feeling the trembling of her muscles beneath the warm flesh. "Why not? You're a beautiful woman, and I think . . . you're attracted to me, right?"

"I . . . do confess that I find myself drawn to you. You are an . . . attractive man."

"Then, can the Mr. Matthews stuff," he said. "I'm Bradley or just Brad if you prefer . . . Eve."

"It will be as you wish, Bradley. Now, I will

go and see to your breakfast." She smiled broadly and turned away.

Bradley made his way to the dining room, taking a table near the window, although there was no traffic outside to observe. Through the window, though, he could see the deep blue, cloudless sky, and the dark green tops of the tall trees that surrounded the town. His inability to recall the nightmare that had caused him to wake up with a silent scream on his lips eased. He lifted the carafe of coffee from the center of the table and poured himself a cup of the steaming hot brew, breathing the heady aroma in deeply. He realized that he'd just been flirting with Eve, and he felt a twinge of guilt. Lena's ashes were upstairs in his duffle bag, and here he was hitting on another woman before he'd even scattered them. *Keep it in your pants, Brad, boy. A little flirting is okay. Lena might even approve. But, nothing beyond that—at least, not yet.*

Sheriff Jason Warfield approached his table just as he was pouring his second cup.

"Good morning, Brad," he said. "Do you mind if I join you?"

"Not at all, sher-, er, Jason," Bradley replied. " I'm waiting for my breakfast. Have you eaten yet?"

"No, as a matter of fact, I have not."

"Then, would you care to join me?"

"I would be honored," Warfield said. "Now, if only Eve would come and take my order."

At that moment, Stark came through the door that Bradley assumed led to the kitchen. She smiled as she approached the table.

"Jason," she said. "I see that you are joining Brad for breakfast. What would you like?"

"I will have whatever he is having," Warfield said.

Without responding, she turned and left.

"You don't even know what I'm having," Bradley said.

"I am sure it will be fine. Ordinarily, Eve does not offer a choice."

Bradley laughed. He felt good inside. It had been so long since he'd felt like laughing. "Yeah, last night, she made me eat whatever the cook prepared. I'll admit, I was a bit surprised when she asked me what I wanted this morning."

"I think it is because she likes you."

"Aw, you're kidding right?"

Warfield looked confused. He screwed his eyes almost shut and furrowed his brow. Then, he smiled. "Ah, kidding? No Brad, I am not . . . kidding. I have not seen her look at a man like she looks at you in . . . well, never actually."

"Oh, wow," Bradley said.

"Do you like her?"

Warfield's question was blunt, and startled Bradley, who almost replied angrily that it was none of his business, until he saw the guilelessness in the man's eyes.

"Well, I just met her, and I'm . . . well, I was . . . married."

"I do not understand. You are no longer married?"

"No, I mean yes. My wife died."

"That is most unfortunate."

Warfield looked so sincere, despite the robotic tone of his response, Bradley couldn't suppress a smile.

` "Why are you smiling?" Warfield asked. "I would think you would be sad about your wife's death."

"I am, I truly am," Bradley said. "But, Lena, my wife, was a person who always believed in looking forward and making the most of the relationships in front of you. Sitting here, talking to you, I realize that she would want me to move on and be happy."

Warfield sat silently for a moment, his head cocked to one side. Then, he smiled. "I think your Lena was a very intelligent person, and you would be intelligent to follow her philosophy of life."

When Eve returned with a tray containing their food, both men snapped their mouths shut. She looked from one to the other, her eyebrows curved upwards, as she placed the plates in front of them.

"And, what were the two of you whispering about?" she asked. "I do hope you were not talking about me."

Bradley felt his cheeks become warm.

Warfield cleared his throat.

"Uh, Bradley was just telling me about his late wife, Lena," Warfield said.

The man might be robotic and seemingly naïve, Bradley thought, but he was fast on his feet. Eve's face creased in a concerned expression as she looked down at Bradley.

"That explains the sad looks that you have so often," she said. "Perhaps a short vacation here in Copper Cove *will* help to ease your loss."

Without waiting for him to respond she turned and walked away. He admired the way she'd reminded him of her invitation to stay without seeming to flirt. Warfield might be guileless, and he might *not* mind Bradley going after a local woman, but he wasn't ready to take a chance on it.

"I think she is right," Warfield said. "This is a peaceful town, and that should help you to come to terms with your grief . . . that, and getting to know Eve better."

The impish look on the man's face caused Bradley to smile again. "Maybe you're right . . . about the peace and quiet, that is." *And, maybe you don't mind me coming on to one of your women. I am definitely not in Kansas anymore, Toto.*

"And the other," Warfield persisted. "Of course, you will have to watch out for Cully."

"What, or who is Cully?"

"Cully Bryant is the mayor of Copper Cove, and he has had his eye on Eve for some time now. Of course, she has no interest in him, so the way is open for your pursuit."

Pursuit wasn't exactly on Bradley's mind, well, it had sort of been on his mind, but he had no intention of being fanatic about it, particularly if a potential rival was part of the picture. The prospect, though, of a peaceful place to plan his future path without Lena at his side was attractive. As for the rest, he would just play it by ear.

Charles Ray

CHAPTER 17

When they finished eating breakfast and had a second cup of coffee each, Warfield said that he had to patrol the town and surrounding areas and took his leave. Eve was nowhere to be seen, leaving Bradley alone in the dining room. He weighed the idea of going back to his room to read, but then decided to explore Copper Cove. If he was going to spend time in the place it would be good to know the lay of the land.

He paused as he stepped through the double doors of the inn, and looked up at the sky. It was bright blue, just as he remembered it being when he first arrived, notwithstanding the gloomy atmosphere on the highway and on the road until they were very near Copper Cove. The streets were also still empty, except for the sheriff's cruiser that he could see turning a corner a block away, and there were no pedestrians.

He stepped off the verandah, stood taking stock for a few moments, and then turned right and headed down, or up, he wasn't sure which way north was, the sidewalk.

The first shop he passed was shuttered, with no sign left to show what it might have been. The next, though, had a sign, *Ye Olde Gift Shoppe,* in Old English script, on a board over the door. Bells over the door tinkled, announcing his entrance. He paused just inside the door and looked around. There were no other customers. A petite woman with her iron grey hair pulled back severely and ending in a bun at the back of her head stood behind the counter at the back of the store. She wore a floor-length grey dress with a white lace collar and lone sleeves that ended in white lace filigree. She smiled at him with thin lips and watery blue eyes as he approached the counter.

"Good morning, welcome to Ye Olde Gift Shoppe," she said in a high pitched voice. "Are you looking for something special, for someone special?"

It sounded like a pitch she'd given thousands of times.

"Uh, I'm just looking around."

"You are new in town. You need to buy a beautiful gift for a beautiful lady, for that special someone."

He was tempted to tell her that *his* lovely lady was dead, but then realized that it would make him sound like a total dickhead. She was just trying to make a living.

"I don't have anyone special at the moment."

She cocked her head and looked up at him, batting incredibly long lashes.

"Really, a handsome man like you must have at least *one* special someone."

Holy shit, she has to be at least sixty, and she's hitting on me. What is it with women in this town? Oh well, don't want to hurt her feelings. "No," he said. "Not really." Avoiding hurting her feelings was one thing, but sharing more than that of himself he wasn't about to do.

She didn't seem to be bothered by his subtle put-off.

"You are staying at the inn," she said. "So, I imagine Eve has set her eyes on you. She likes them tall, dark and handsome."

The conversation was moving too fast in the wrong direction. Bradley decided the wise thing to do was move on.

"Ms. Stark is a nice looking woman," he said. "But, I can assure you, she is not interested in me."

The look on her face told Bradley with no uncertainty that she knew he was lying. He began backing toward the exit. "I, uh, don't really see anything here that interests me," he said. "Sorry. I was just looking around. I'd better be going on . . . nice meeting you."

As the door closed behind him, he could hear her laughing over the tinkling of the bells.

What a strange town, he thought. He'd only met four of its residents, and each one seemed stranger than the one before, the tiny lady in the gift shop the zaniest of all. He continued his walk along the sidewalk, passing other shops without taking much notice of their wares or whether or not they were inhabited.

As he neared the end of the sidewalk, which stopped abruptly at a verge of green that stretched out toward the towering trees that seemed to ring the entire town, he saw a slightly overweight, short, middle-aged man on the sidewalk across the street. He raised his hand in a greeting, but the man averted his gaze and ducked into a building. *Strange; that's the first unfriendly person I've seen here.*

He shrugged and stepped off the sidewalk onto the grass, feeling the spongy earth beneath his feet. Straight ahead for a few hundred yards was a wall of trees, their dark green foliage reaching for the deep blue sky. Beneath them, all he could see was dark shadows. He looked left. More trees, about two football fields away, and just short of the trees he saw a greyish structure, a building of some kind. His curiosity aroused, he set out in that direction.

As he drew closer, he could see that the structure was an old church, a stone building with a bell tower at the peak of the steeply sloped roof, and large, dark wooden double doors at the top of steep stone steps in the front. The church had been white at some time in the past, but time had faded the paint to a light grey which was smeared with greenish mold under the eaves of the roof. Large arched windows with stained glass panes flanked the doors.

On the ground beside the steps he saw what appeared at first to be a bundle of old rags. When he was about ten feet from it, the pile suddenly moved, causing him to stop and stare open-mouthed. He prepared to run as the pile began rising up, but stopped when he saw that it was an old man dressed in filthy, ragged clothing that hung off his emaciated frame in tatters.

Bradley and the old man stood there for a minute staring at each other. The man's mouth gaped open showing gaps where teeth were missing, and brown, crooked stubs that once upon a time had been healthy teeth. At first his light brown eyes didn't seem to focus, but when they did, they opened wide. His mouth flopped open and snapped shut.

"Hello," Bradley said. "Who are you?"

In response to Bradley's greeting, the old man opened his mouth wide and shrieked. It was a shrill sound like a tin whistle. He then turned on his heels and fled around the side of the church, running pell mell toward the trees until he disappeared in the gloomy shadows.

"This town just keeps getting stranger and stranger," Bradley said to himself.

Charles Ray

CHAPTER 18

After his near encounter with the old man at the church, Bradley decided it might be best to return to the inn. Eve was at her place behind the reception desk when he entered.

"Welcome back, Bradley," she said as he approached the desk. "Did you enjoy your exploration of Copper Cove?"

"It's an interesting place, but I didn't see many people."

"Ours is not a large community. I believe we have a population of one hundred and fifty souls."

Bradley tried to picture that. Some of the classes he taught had almost that many students, and the auditorium he occasionally used for his lectures seated four hundred. He could just imagine the population of Copper Cove being lost among a sea of students.

"Did you get an opportunity to talk to

anyone?" she asked him.

"Well, there was the lady who runs the gift shop."

"Ah yes, that would be Esmerelda. You would be well advised to watch out when in her presence. She can be quite devious. Did you meet anyone else?"

"No, there was a man on the sidewalk, but when I tried to talk to him, he seemed to be avoiding me," he said. "Oh, and there was a really strange old man out by the church."

Her face paled, and a hand went to her throat. "Y-you did not go inside the church did you?"

"Uh, no, I just approached the building, and I saw this ragged old tramp. But, when I approached him, he screamed and ran off into the woods."

"You must p-promise me, Bradley, that you will under no circumstances enter the church."

The tension in her voice was palpable.

"Well, sure, but what's the problem? It's just an old building."

"Trust me. It is quite dangerous. I would not want anything to happen to you."

"Yeah, sure, I'll stay out of the old church. Now, what about the old geezer I saw?"

"You must also stay away from him."

"Why? He looked dirty, but harmless. What is he, some kind of serial killer or something?"

She came from behind the desk and

grabbed his hands pulling them against her chest. He could feel the soft swell of her breasts and the warmth of her skin beneath the silk blouse she wore, and up so close the scent of her lavender soap aroused him. "Bradley, promise me you will stay away from that man. He is not a . . . serial killer, but he is very dangerous. Promise me you will stay away from him . . . *and* that you will not enter the church."

He squeezed her hand and smiled down at her.

"Okay, I promise," he said. "I'll stay away from the church, and I'll avoid the old man."

She let out a breath. "Good. Now, it is time for lunch. Go and wash up, and by the time you come back down I will have your lunch ready."

As he made his way to his room he thought it odd that at the last she had almost sounded like Lena.

Charles Ray

CHAPTER 19

Eve stayed close to Bradley for the rest of the day, joining him for lunch, insisting that he keep her company in the reception area and entertain her with more stories of the 'outside,' and joining him again for supper.

Warfield came to the inn just as they were finishing supper and invited Bradley to join him and some others for a card game at the town hall, which also served as the sheriff's office and community center. Like a mother hen, Eve objected, but the combined arguments of Bradley and the sheriff wore her down.

As they were leaving the inn, Warfield said, "Do not worry, Eve, we will take good care of him. If he is to stay here, he should get to know other people."

"Yes, I suppose you are right," she said.

Bradley didn't miss the look that passed between them, but he also didn't understand it.

The two men walked the two blocks to the town hall. The card game was being held in the community center, a large room on the ground floor. There were two men waiting for them; Philo the mechanic and the middle aged man who had avoided Bradley earlier. Warfield introduced him as Cully Bryant, mayor of Copper Cove.

"Pleased to meet you, Mr. Mayor," Bradley said.

"We do not stand on ceremony here," Bryant said. "Just call me Cully." His tone of voice, however, was not welcoming.

Bradley was reminded of the in-crowd kids he'd encountered in high school, or the snobby Greek letter types in college, who could make the warmest welcome speech sound like an insult or a challenge. In Bryant's case he heard a definite challenge.

He was determined, though, not to respond directly to that challenge. Over the years he'd developed his own method for dealing with Bryant's type. "Glad to meet you Cully," he said. "My friends call me Bradley or Brad. How're things going with you, Philo?"

"Aw, not too bad," the mechanic replied. "Still no word on the part for your car, though, so I reckon that counts as bad news, eh?"

"No problem. I'm starting to enjoy my stay here in Copper Cove. There are some . . . interesting people."

He looked at Bryant. The subtle meaning of his words, he could see from the two spots of color on the man's cheeks, hadn't been lost. *So, you want to play circle jerk games with me, do you? Want to show off with mine's bigger than yours games? Well, friend, bring it on.*

The tension between Bradley and Bryant was obviously not lost on Warfield either. He sat and began opening a fresh deck of cards. "Bradley, have you ever played Texas Hold 'Em Poker?" he asked.

Bradley sat to Warfield's left and Philo sat to his left, leaving him facing Bryant, who continued to give him the evil eye.

"No, never have," he said. "I assume it's not too different from regular poker."

Bryant snickered. Warfield gave him a stern look.

"Now, Cully it is not nice to treat a guest like that." He turned back to Bradley. "It is similar to stud poker, but there some special variations which I will explain to you. I learned this game a few months ago during a visit to Upper Marlboro. It is very interesting, and most entertaining, and very easy to learn. I taught Cully and Philo in one evening." He shuffled the cards. "First, the buy-in for our friendly game is twenty dollars."

Bradley couldn't suppress a smile. Warfield sounded like he was lecturing to a group of grade schoolers, explaining a new playground game.

As Bradley reached for his wallet, Bryant snorted. "Is that too much for you?"

Bradley wasn't fond of gambling, but he'd played in small stakes games when he was in college, mostly draw or stud poker, and on occasion dominos, so he'd expected to have to pay to play. With what Eve was charging him for the room, which included food, he could easily spare a twenty if it meant making friends with these men—with the exception of Cully Bryant, who he was beginning to dislike a lot.

"No, it's not too much," he said, addressing Warfield. He took a twenty from his wallet and laid it on the table.

Philo and Warfield did the same. Bryant, looking disappointed, hesitated, but finally also put a twenty on the table. Warfield counted out chips, explaining that the blue chips were ten dollars, the red ones were five, and the white ones were one. Bradley got one blue, one red, and five whites, which he stacked neatly to his right.

"Very well," Warfield said. "Now, I will explain how the game is played. First, the player to the right of the dealer, if I am dealer, that would be Cully, cuts the shuffled deck of cards, and each player is given two cards, face down. These are known as the hole cards. After the hole cards are dealt, the player to the left of the dealer bets by paying what is known as a small blind. In our games that is one dollar. The next player plays a large blind which is two dollars. Then, the dealer discards the next card in the deck and places three cards on the table, face up. The player left of the large blind starts the betting. Then, one card is discarded and a card is put face up next to the first three, and betting begins again, and then a final deal of a throwaway, which is called a burn card, and a fifth face up card, and final betting. The player with the best hand wins what is on the table. Is that clear?"

Bradley was trying hard to remember everything Warfield had said. He was pretty confident that, even though he might make a few missteps in the first hand or two, he would get it eventually. "Yeah, I think I have it," he said.

To show that he'd been listening, Bradley placed a one dollar chip in the center of the table. Philo smiled and placed two white chips next to Bradley's chip. Warfield smiled, nodded, and dealt each of them two cards, and the game began.

A smirking Bryant won the first hand with two pair, Kings and Tens, mainly from the King and Ten on the table, and matching cards in his hand. Bradley hadn't made any mistakes, so Warfield passed the deck to him.

"It is your turn to deal," he said.

"This is an interesting town you have here," Bradley said as he dealt the first cards.

Warfield picked up his cards, glanced at

them, then put them back on the table face down. "In what way do you find it interesting?" he asked.

Bradley lifted the corners of his cards. He'd dealt himself the Kings of Diamonds and Spades. "Well, just about everyone here is pretty friendly." He looked pointedly across the table at Bryant. "But, when I was walking out near the old church building, I came across this old fellow who seemed frightened of me. He screamed and ran into the woods." As he spoke, Bradley tossed a burn card face down in the center of the table and then dealt three cards face up, a Two of Spades, King of Hearts, and Six of Spades.

"Bet's to you, Jason," Philo said. "That sounds like old man Paxton."

Warfield looked again at his hole cards. He frowned. "Check," he said. "Yes, I would say that you are correct. Harry Paxton does live in the forest near the church."

"I'll bet two dollars," Bradley said. "What is he, some kind of mental patient or something?"

"Call," said Philo. "He is a crazy old coot, that's for sure, but I don't think he's ever been in an asylum."

"Call," Bryant said with a grumpy tone in his voice.

"I also call. He is an eccentric old man, not a mental patient. You should be more considerate of your fellow man, Philo." Warfield's voice carried no sting. He spoke in such a matter of fact manner, he could have well have been describing the weather.

Bradley tossed another burn card and dealt the fourth face up card, the King of Clubs. He fought to keep his expression neutral. "Eccentric is hardly sufficient to describe him," he said. "He's dressed like a scarecrow, and he acted like he'd seen the devil himself when I approached him. Bet's on me, I bet two dollars."

Philo called the bet, and Bryant, after peering yet again at his cards for a long time, finally called. Warfield looked at Bradley instead of his cards.

"Did he say anything to you? Oh, I call by the way."

"Pot's right," Bradley said. "No, he just screamed and ran away. What's his story?"

The fifth and final card, an Ace, was face up on the table. There was silence as everyone stared at it. Finally, Philo bet two dollars. Bryant covered his bet and raised two dollars. Bradley wondered what cards the man held that might beat the four Kings he was looking at. Warfield tossed four dollars into the pot, calling Bryant.

"Harry is a troubled soul," Warfield said. "It is best to stay away from him. He does not have a history of violence, but we have not had strangers in Copper Cove, so there is no way of knowing how he will react to you."

"We know one way," Bradley said. "He ran like hell. I guess he's never seen a black man before. By the way, I see the four dollars and raise two." A slight widening of Bryant's eyes pleased him. He was beginning to think the man was bluffing.

"Yeah," Philo said. "You're the first Ne-, er, black person to ever come to Copper Cove, so it might've startled him. I don't think he's ever been outside the town in his life. I'm out. The pot's done got too rich for me." He turned his cards upside down and tossed them into the center of the table.

Bryant's face was contorted in a sneering expression as he shoved a blue chip into the center. "I will see your two and raise it another three."

Warfield looked at Bryant through narrowed slits. "I think I will do as Philo and throw my cards in," he said. "It would appear that we have two players with good hands . . . or two fools. Only time will tell."

Bradley gazed steadily at Bryant. He saw a muscle twitch under the man's left eye. *He's bluffing.* He pushed all of his remaining chips into the center of the table. "I believe the expression is 'I'm all in,' so it's now up to you," he said. "If you think your hand beats mine, it'll cost you most of what you have there."

Bryant's face was a study in emotions, but the one that Bradley thought was most clear was hate. He made a growling sound deep in his throat and flipped his cards face down onto the table. "It would appear that the pot is yours," he said.

Bradley tossed his cards face down into the pile and raked in the chips. His luck changed with that one winning hand. Warfield and Philo were cautious players, so it took him several hands to win their chips. Bryant, on the other hand, tried two more times to bluff him with weak hands, losing each time, so that he was forced to either buy more chips or sit out. He sat out the last three hands, glaring at Bradley across the table.

At the end, with everyone's chips in front of him, Bradley cashed in.

"Thank you gentlemen," he said as he folded the four twenties and placed them in his wallet. "It's been an interesting, and profitable evening."

"You are quite skillful at cards," Warfield said. "I do believe you have played this game before."

"Not this specific game, but I was a pretty fair seven-card stud player in college. The rules are a little different, but the strategy is the same."

Warfield and Philo took their defeat in stride, a low stakes game for amusement, but Bryant continued to sulk.

"One more thing, Bradley," Warfield said. "I do advise you to avoid the area around the church. As I said, I do not know how Harry Paxton will react to you, and I would not want you to be hurt while you are a guest in our town."

"Yes," Bryant chimed in. "It is not a good idea to do too much nosing around where you do not belong."

Warfield's warning had sounded well-intentioned, but Bryant's sounded more like a threat. Bradley didn't like being threatened. He turned to Warfield. "I'll certainly keep your advice in mind."

The sheriff responded with a good natured smile. "Good. It has been a most pleasant evening, gentlemen. We must do this again soon."

"Yeah, only next time, I'm gonna clean this fella out," Philo said. He jabbed Bradley in the shoulder with a stubby forefinger. "And, that means you, Bradley."

"You just might," Bradley said. "You never know how the cards will fall."

As they were leaving, Bryant edged close to Bradley and leaned in toward him until his lips nearly touched his ear. "I advise you to stay from Eve Stark, Matthews," he whispered harshly. "She is *not* for you."

Before Bradley could respond, he pushed past and rushed out of the room. Now *that*, Bradley thought, was clearly a threat—worse, it was an order. He didn't like being threatened, and he didn't like being told what he could or couldn't do.

CHAPTER 20

It was dark and the building was quiet when Bradley arrived back at the inn. A single lamp on the reception desk lit the lobby. Widely spaced sconces on the walls illuminated the stairwell and hallway. He assumed that Eve had already turned in, so he went directly to his room.

His sleep was restless: the things he'd been told at the card game—especially Bryant's veiled threat; for that was how Bradley viewed it—kept tumbling through his mind. He woke up the next morning to do something about the challenges that had been set, or at least one of them.

He found Eve Stark in the lobby. She had a distracted look on her face, so Bradley decided to put Harry Paxton, the old derelict, at the top of his to-do list.

He walked past her without saying anything and went into the dining room, where he sat at what he was coming to view as his usual table. After a few minutes, Eve followed him in.

"So, what will you have for breakfast this fine Saturday morning?" she asked. She smiled at him, the distracted look he'd noticed in the lobby now absent.

"Why don't you surprise me," he responded. "I plan to do a lot of walking this morning, so I'll need the energy."

Her brow wrinkled. "I do hope that you are not planning on another trip to the old church. That would be most unwise."

He didn't like lying to her. He didn't like lying to anyone. But, he didn't want an argument, and he knew that she would argue with him if he told her what he was planning to do. Since she was number two on his to-do list, he felt it prudent to stay on her good side.

"No, I have no intention of going there," he said. "I thought I'd explore the rest of the town; maybe get to know a few more of the people. I didn't see much yesterday and I've only met four people—other than the old man I saw at the church, and he hardly counts."

She looked skeptical, but he looked at her without flinching, and she finally relaxed and sighed.

"Very well, then, you wait here, and I shall bring you a special breakfast."

After breakfast, she walked him out to the verandah, brushing her shoulder lightly against his arm all the way. Once on the verandah, she stood there, forcing him to start his exploration in the opposite direction of the one he actually intended. He crossed the street, walking slowly and pretending to be interested in the things in the windows of the buildings he passed, but actually watching the inn reflected in the glass of the windows. When he saw her go back inside the inn, he ducked into the alley and made his way along the service road behind the buildings in the direction of the church, hoping than no one would mistake him for a prowler and shoot at him.

After five minutes the church came into view. He cut across a weed-choked expanse of ground, and was soon standing looking up at the weather-worn doors of the church. The old man was nowhere to be seen. Bradley walked around the side of the building, toward the decrepit looking graveyard with its moldy, oddly tilting headstones at the edge of the woods. He made a mental note to come back another time and explore the graveyard. Old cemeteries fascinated him, and it might, he thought, give him an idea for topics to have his students write about. A few yards beyond the graveyard, he saw the old man sitting with his back against a tree, looking up at the sky.

Not wanting to startle him, Bradley slowly worked his way into the trees beyond the graveyard, and moved quietly in his direction. When he was six feet away, he stepped out of the trees into the sunlight. His shadow stopped just short of the old man's feet.

The old man's eyes opened wide, and his shirt made a rasping noise against the rough bark of the tree as he scrambled to stand. He held his hands up, groping like a blind man in unfamiliar territory.

"No, no," he cried. "Please don't hurt me. Stay away, demon, stay away."

"I won't hurt you, Harry Paxton," Bradley said softly.

"H-how do you k-know my name?"

"Sheriff Warfield, Jason, told me. He's a friend of mine."

The old man's quivering eased, but only a little. Bradley stood stock still to avoid spooking him.

"I know t-the sheriff. He's a g-good man. Who are you?"

"My name's Bradley Matthews."

"Y-you're not from C-copper C-c-cove. Are you a freeman?"

Bradley shook his head. Even the demented old coot spoke in riddles. He was a puzzle, just like the rest of the town. He decided, though, to play along.

"Yeah, yeah I am. My car broke down on the highway, and the sheriff, Jason, had it towed here to be repaired. I'm just staying here until that's done. I take it you're a native of Copper Cove?"

"Yes, no." Paxton scratched at the wild grey stubble on his cheeks and ran a grubby hand through his unkempt grey hair. "I m-mean, I wasn't born here or nothin'. I come here sort of like you, by accident, and I been here ever since."

"How long has that been?"

Paxton scratched his head again. "Uh, I don't rightly remember. A long time, a real long time, that's for sure."

"Where are you from originally?"

"Uh, I . . . I don't remember that either."

Wow, this guy's gone completely around the bend. Oh well, I at least talked to him, and he seems harmless, so the next thing is to see if Eve's really interested. "Well, look," Bradley said. "It's been nice talking to you, but I have to go now."

"Where you going?" The old man moved forward, reaching out toward Bradley. "Can't you stay and talk to me for a spell?"

"I can't stay long. Eve will be expecting me for lunch."

"Eve?" Paxton looked puzzled. "Is that Eve Stark? Lady that runs the inn?"

"Yes, that's her, but I guess you know her, right?"

Paxton got a faraway look in his eyes. "Uh-huh, I do . . . you look like a nice young fella, so I'll tell you something. But, you have to promise not to tell anybody I told you."

"Sure, what is it," Bradley said.

The old man leaned in close, so close that Bradley could smell his sour breath and funky body odor. "You promise, you won't tell?"

"Yes, I promise."

"There's two things in Copper Creek you have to stay far away from," the old man whispered. "One of 'em is Devil's Lake. It didn't get that name by accident. The devil himself lives in that dark water."

"What's the other?" Bradley asked.

"The other is Eve Stark."

"Wha-" But, before Bradley could finish, the old man whirled around and dashed into the woods, moving so rapidly he was out of sight before Bradley could react.

Rather than chase after him through the woods, and risk possibly tripping over a fallen tree branch and hurting himself, and then be left there for wolves or some other wild thing to ravage his defenseless body, Bradley decided to go back to the inn to work on the next item on his list.

CHAPTER 21

Eve was sitting in a white rattan chair on the verandah when Bradley walked up the sidewalk to the inn. A matching chair, empty, sat across from her, and a glass-topped rattan table sat between. A large glass pitcher containing a yellowish liquid and ice cubes, and two empty glasses sat on the table. Bradley felt a twinge of guilt, and wondered if she would figure out that he'd lied to her. He looked intently at her for any sign that she might be upset, but the smile she beamed at him seemed full of nothing but warmth.

"I thought you might be thirsty after your exploration," she said as he mounted the steps. "So, I prepared a pitcher of lemonade. I think it is such a lovely idea, sitting on the verandah and sipping lemonade, do you not agree?" She made no mention of the fact that he'd been coming from the direction of the church. Whether she suspected or not, he couldn't tell from her expression, but it didn't seem so.

He dropped himself into the empty chair. "Lemonade sounds like a great idea. Should I pour?"

"Why, thank you, sir," she said. When she smiled at him two dimples formed to either side of her mouth. "You are quite the gentleman today."

"It's easy to be a gentleman when there is such a beautiful lady to be served," he said.

Her response to his flirtatious remark was the appearance of two round red spots on her cheeks and a lowering of her gaze to the table top. He filled a glass and slid it toward her. As she reached for it, he let his hand lightly brush hers. He felt a spark like that you get after rubbing your shoes on a carpet and then touching a metal door knob. She twitched, but did not jerk her hand away.

"Thank you," she said quietly.

He filled the other glass and took a sip from it. The sweet-tart taste was refreshing after his morning walk, and he *had* in fact been thinking about lemonade during his walk back to the inn. He wondered if, along with her other eccentricities, she was a mind reader. That, though, would be a question to be answered later. Now, in addition to seducing her, he needed information. The problem would be accomplishing both tasks. He had the sense that she didn't like being interrogated about the history of Copper Cove. Then, he remembered something Lena had once told him. "Women are truly impressed by a man who is honest," she'd said during a commercial break in a TV show they'd been watching. "She might be upset at it, but in the end, a man who tells a woman the truth is the man she trusts, and trust is the most important element in a relationship." It was a long shot, but he decided to give it a try.

"Eve . . . I . . . have a confession to make," he said.

She looked at him over the top of her glass. "You went to the church again?" Her voice was quiet and without emotion.

"Uh, well . . . I know I promised not to, but I was curious."

She laughed quietly, a throaty laugh, deep in her throat. "I knew that you would. You, Bradley Matthews, are a curious person. When you set your mind to a problem, you are unable to resist . . . how do you put it . . . nosing about. So, what did you discover?"

"I met that old guy, Harry Paxton," he said. "He's a nutter, for sure, but basically, he seems harmless."

"Hm, yes, I suppose he is harmless, but you can never be sure with people like that. So, what did the two of you talk about?"

He knew without knowing how he knew that the subject of Devil's Lake would be a sensitive one. "He, uh, warned me to stay away from some place called Devil's Lake."

Even knowing it would be sensitive, he

wasn't prepared for her reaction. Her face paled. The glass of lemonade she was holding stopped inches away from her lips.

"D-devil's Lake? What did he tell you about Devil's Lake?" She leaned forward, and Bradley could tell from the waves in her glass that her hand was shaking.

"Nothing that made sense," he said. "I mean, he said the devil himself lived in the lake, and that I should stay far away from it. Now, how crazy is that, right?"

She swallowed hard as she put her glass down and put her now free hand to her breast. After a few deep breaths, she looked deeply into his eyes.

"Harry Paxton is a demented old fool. There is no devil in Devil's Lake. It is, however, dangerous. There are snakes, and the bottom is very soft and dotted with pockets of quicksand, so there is a danger of a person wading being sucked under and drowning. No one from Copper Cove goes anywhere near it for that reason and I suggest that you follow his advice. In that, at least, he is correct. It is dangerous." Her voice was hard and her expression was stormy.

He held his hands up in a placating gesture. "Don't worry, I'm not a fan of water sports, and I've never been fishing in my life. I have no intention of exploring the lake. I am curious, though. How did it get its name?"

She relaxed then and sat back in her chair.

"It is an interesting story, actually. The

lake got its name before the first European settlers came to the area. The local Indian tribe, the Piscataway, called it the Lake of the Devil because according to their tribal myth, it is the home of evil water spirits that trapped and ate any of their tribe who strayed too close to the shore. Even though they were fishermen, they never fished from the lake." She picked her glass up and took a dainty sip. "The first settlers here came from England in 1590. According to legend, after two children drowned in the lake, they too declared it forbidden and adopted the Indian name."

"Okay, okay, you've convinced me. Devil's Lake is hereby *off* my itinerary."

She wiggled her brows and smiled impishly at him. "So, what do you plan to do for the rest of your day?"

He looked at his watch. "Well, it's almost lunchtime," he said. "I thought I'd grab a light lunch and go to my room. Maybe I'll read a bit or take a nap until supper."

"That is a very good idea. I was planning a special supper for you tonight. A special . . . private supper."

"Now, that sounds like a good idea, but since I'm the only guest, what other kind of supper *would* we have?"

She stood and put her hands on her hips, looking down at him from beneath half-lowered lids. "I said it was a *special* supper. For now I will say no more. You must wait and see. Now, go into the dining room and I will bring you your lunch. As for supper . . . I will see you in your room at seven." With a swish of her skirt and a tantalizing swing of her hips she strode away.

Now, that sounds promising. I wonder if that's what the old man was talking about. He looked up at the sky. *I'm sorry, Lena. I still truly love you, and only you, but I guess I'm only human after all.*

CHAPTER 22

In his misty prison, he brooded. *If he'd had corporeal form, as he'd had so many generations past, he would have been sitting with his head cradled in his hands. All he had left now was his name, Ahnok, a name that had caused mortals and demigods alike to tremble in abject terror at one time, and his ability to project his will on others, but only over a short span of distance. Once, long ago, he and his brothers had been able to control vast populations of mortals over great distances.*

Thinking of his brothers changed his brooding mood to one of white hot anger, an anger that boiled from deep within his evanescent essence until it seemed to threaten to evaporate him and wipe him from existence. Oh, how they had betrayed him! But, they would pay. They would all pay.

They had inhabited the land for a long time, long before the first humans came; Ahnok and his kind had been there for so long they had forgotten when they came, or from whence. They had no name for themselves, for there were no others but them, and when you are the only being in a place, you are just . . . you. As individuals, they had names, of course, as there was still the need for individuals to distinguish themselves from others. Over time, many drifted away, seeking other diversions, until in this place there were only three left; Ahnok and his three brothers, Chipiapa, Susqua, and Shinoo, and a sister, the youngest, Lenapi. They spent their time frolicking among the flora and fauna, soaring through the air, and playing tricks upon each other. They did not know night or day; the passage of time bore no meaning, and except for the unique weakness of each, had nothing to fear.

They were immortals—of a sort. They lived, well, forever, but each had a weak point, a substance that could, would, end existence. For Chipiapa it was the sap of the pine tree, which could burn and bubble him into a puddle of goo if he was unfortunate, or foolish enough to allow it to come into contact with his skin. Susqua could be consumed by fire, so whenever lightning ignited the trees or underbrush, he fled deep into the caves in the hills until the fire burned itself out. Shinoo was deathly allergic to the juice of the mulberry, but the noxious plant was easy to identify and smelly, so even the birds refused to eat it. Lenapi's weakness was the secretion from a species of frog that lived in the swamps, so she never entered boggy areas. But, it was Ahnok, the youngest of the four demigods, who had the most debilitating weakness. He could not cross a body of water, not even a shallow spring. Whenever he came near the water, he could feel his strength being sucked away, and knew that should he immerse himself in the water, he would shrivel up and blow away on the breeze. They roamed over the land, but Ahnok was careful to avoid those places with bodies of water, avoiding even small puddles after rains.

Time flowed and they amused themselves until the humans came. The swarthy people who called themselves Piscataway and Susquehannock, and who lived in long houses made of poles and bark, were at first a source of amusement for Ahnok and his siblings to observe.

"We should not interfere or interact with them," Chipiapa, the eldest said. "They are different from us. They are fragile and they do not live long. Contact with us would be dangerous for them."

Ahnok, though, was curious about these fragile beings, and would spend more time than his siblings watching them. It was he who discovered that they were able to insert thoughts into the humans' minds, and even inhabit their bodies and make them do whatever they wanted. He would often amuse himself by doing just that. Over time, it became addictive. He experienced a thrill like nothing he'd ever known. The sense of power it gave him was indescribable.

Then, Chipiapa found out what he'd been doing. He and the others confronted Ahnok deep in the forest one day.

"You must cease this immediately," Chipiapa said. "We must not interfere in the affairs of these humans."

"But, brother," Ahnok protested. "They are weak and we are strong. Besides, I do them no harm. When I possess them I give them the ability to do things they would otherwise not be able to do."

"But, it is wrong," Lenapi said. "They may be short-lived, but they do not deserve to be treated thus."

They argued back and forth until Ahnok promised to cease his interference into the affairs of the humans, a promise he broke often when he thought the others were not paying attention.

Things came to a head after the others, the humans with pale skin and strange clothing, came to the region. Ahnok's possession of a local warrior allowed him to learn that the strangers came to the region from lands far *across the ocean called England and France, two groups of pale skinned ones who fought with each other, and who enlisted the swarthy ones in their wars. Unlike the ones the newcomers called Indians for some reason, these pale-faced ones fought with weapons that spit fire and sent pellets and balls of metal flying through the air to rip their enemies apart, instead of tomahawks, arrows, and spears, which were deadly in close combat, but ineffective at the ranges available to these amazing weapons.*

Ahnok was fascinated, and after entering the mind of one of the English decided these new humans were better subjects for his explorations. His siblings mostly ignored the affairs of humans, so they were unaware at first of his change in habits.

It was only after a particularly vicious battle in which an Indian village was burned to the ground by the English force and all of its occupants slaughtered that Chipiapa discovered that the commander of the English had been possessed by Ahnok.

As the eldest, Chipiapa called a council deep within the forest, and commanded Ahnok's presence, a summons that Ahnok dared not resist.

"Ahnok," Chipiapa said. "You have broken your vow. You continue to involve yourself with these humans, and worse, you use your power over them to engage in activities that are not appropriate."

Defiant, Ahnok drew himself up and glared at his brother.

"These humans are a bloodthirsty lot. They kill each other with or without my intervention. I merely make it more efficient, and more interesting."

Susqua, he who could be harmed by fire, had fire in his eyes. The second oldest, he did not have the patience of his older brother.

"You know that we are not supposed to interact with the humans," he said. "Their puny brains are not equipped to deal with us."

"Who made such a foolish rule?" Ahnok demanded. "We are the superior being. Why should these puny entities not serve us? As the hare becomes food for the hawk, we should view them thus."

"Food, you view them as food?" Lenapi's tone was one of incredulity.

"In a way, that is exactly what they are, they are food for my psyche. They entertain me. Am I not entitled to my entertainment?"

Chipiapa made a snorting sound. Rising up to his full height, which towered half a meter above the top of Ahnok's head, he glowered down at his younger brother.

"Your entertainment, little brother, tends unfortunately to the bloody and violent. I have noticed that many of your little . . . entertainments end up dead."

Ahnok shrugged. "It is not my fault that they are so fragile. Besides, there are so many of them, the loss of a few is insignificant."

Chipiapa sputtered. The others looked at him with mouths agape.

"You, you are mad," Chipiapa said. "They are living beings. This is not the way we treat living creatures."

"They are inferior," Ahnok said. "They deserve no better treatment than the animals we slaughter for food . . . less in fact, as they do not even provide nourishment."

With his brow furrowed, Chipiapa lowered his head. His right hand, resting on his muscular thigh, trembled.

"I had hoped it would not come to this, little brother," he said. He sighed deeply. "But, you leave me . . . us no choice."

Chipiapa raised his right hand. Before Ahnok realized the significance of the gesture, Susqua and Shinoo sprang forward and seized him, pinning his arms against his body. Ahnok was a demigod, a being of immense strength, physical and mental, and no human, no army of humans could stand against him. But, against two of his own kind, he was helpless. He struggled, but to no avail.

"Unhand me," he screamed. "You cannot do this to me."

Chipiapa put his face close to Ahnok's. "Not only can we, my brother, but we must. You have violated all that we stand for. You are no longer fit to be among us."

He stepped aside and nodded toward Lenapi, who stepped up to face Ahnok.

"I am truly sorry, dear brother," she said.

"But, you have left us no other choice."

Ordinarily, Ahnok would not be overwhelmed mentally—it was not something that had been done before—but, the combined power of four determined minds sent him hurtling into blackness.

—––

Thinking back to that day, now more than three centuries past, he remembered waking up after being unconscious for how long he had no idea. When the light returned to his eyes, he'd felt strange, and when he reached up to rub at his eyes, he screamed. He could not feel his eyes. He saw the four of them, standing there looking down at him, expressions of immense sadness on their faces.

Then, Chipiapa explained what had happened. They had removed his essence from the physical form it occupied, and brought him to an island in the middle of a lake. The separation of his spirit and body was an unnecessary insult, because he could not cross the water, but no matter how he'd begged, they'd been unmoved.

They were not, however, completely without mercy. Near the lake was a small settlement of Englishmen called Copper Cove. Chipiapa had made it possible for Ahnok to feed off the energy of these humans, and to control them to a limited degree. But, he'd also planted in the minds of the humans a dread fear of the lake, basing it on the Indian lore about the evil water spirits in the water. That fear was reinforced by the sensations people received from Ahnok's power emanations whenever they were near the lake.

And thus, for three hundred years had Ahnok suffered his exile. The population serving him rarely exceeded two hundred souls. The town had faded over the centuries, and had become somewhat inbred. Seldom did outsiders venture there, and the natives seldom went outside. Only when absolutely necessary did anyone leave, and they didn't stay away long. But, Ahnok had not wasted those centuries. Whenever anyone did leave Copper Cove, upon their return, Ahnok drained their memory of everything they'd seen and heard. And, he learned. His range extended. For brief moments he could reach out two hundred miles. He had made a plan. And, that plan was about to come to fruition.

Soon, very soon now, he would leave this island. He would again walk among the humans, and they would amuse him. But, before doing that, he would seek out his treacherous siblings.

And. They. Would. Pay.

Charles Ray

CHAPTER 23

After returning to his room, Bradley had read for an hour, but he'd fallen asleep in the middle of a chapter. At 6:00 pm he awoke lying on top of the bedclothes with the book across his chest.

His groggy mind at first didn't know where he was, and the strangeness of the room startled him. But, as his vision cleared, so did his thoughts and he remembered. Copper Cove, the strangest place, with the weirdest bunch of people, and he had a date with one of them. He glanced at his watch. *Holy crap, I' only have an hour to get ready.*

He rolled quickly off the bed.

It took him less than an hour to get ready, only forty minutes in fact. When he heard the soft tapping on his door at a few minutes to seven, he was sitting on the two-cushioned sofa in the corner of the room with the unread book on his lap.

"It's not locked," he said.

The door swung inward, and Eve Stark

followed a wheeled cart into the room. Two plates, a bottle of red wine in a silver urn, two glasses, and the requisite amount of silverware sat atop a glistening white linen table cloth covering the cart. The aroma of breaded pork chops, broccoli smothered in cheese, and golden brown cloverleaf rolls wafted across the room and caused Bradley's mouth to water. But, the sight of her caused his mouth to drop open.

The shift, chemise, or whatever the appropriate name was for the flimsy cloth that draped her curvaceous body, he wasn't sure, nor did he particularly care. What drew his attention was the way it shifted and swung as she moved, caressing and exposing every curve of her body, and while it wasn't even semi-transparent, it might as well have been, the way it limned her form for his greedy eyes.

She didn't miss the way he devoured her with his eyes. Little circles of red appeared on her cheeks.

"I hope everything is to your liking," she said.

He had to swallow a couple of times before he could find his voice. "Everything looks great," he said. "My compliments to the chef; if the food tastes as good as it smells, it'll be fantastic."

She smiled and did a slight curtsy.

"Thank you, kind sir. I decided that in order to make this a very special dinner, I would cook everything myself."

"So, not only beautiful and sexy, but she can cook."

He was rewarded with reddened cheeks and fluttering lashes.

"Do you really think I am beautiful?" Her hands trembled as she picked up the bottle of wine.

He placed his hand over hers, feeling the trembling and the warmth that came off her skin like the heat from a radiator.

"Of course I think you're beautiful," he said. "You're a very beautiful woman."

She lowered her gaze and continued pouring the wine. She sat next to him and lifted her glass.

"You too are a beautiful person, Bradley," she said. "You are the most beautiful person I have ever seen."

Bradley removed his hand, not so fast it might make her think he was pulling away from her. He'd wanted to, though. Sure, he'd been flirting with her, but he'd been expecting her to demur, not flirt back. He was beginning to have second thoughts about the whole thing. Lena hadn't been dead that long. He wasn't really ready for this. *It was that damn Cully Bryant poking at me. Sure, she's beautiful, and under other circumstances I'd jump her bones in a minute, but this is wrong.* "Say, why don't we eat this fantastic meal before it gets cold," he said.

She frowned. "I suppose you're right," she

said.

They ate in silence. The food *was* good. When the last pork chop and bit of broccoli was gone, and they'd sopped up the last of the juice with the last piece of roll, Bradley lounged back in his chair and rubbed his stomach.

"That was just about the best meal I've had in a long time." He wasn't lying. Lena had been a good cook, but nowhere near this good. This was the kind of meal you got in restaurants so classy they didn't put prices on the menu. "You should move to the city and open your own restaurant. Serving food like this, you'd become famous . . . and rich."

She wiped daintily at her lips with a linen napkin. Bradley noticed a smudge of pink lipstick just under her lower lip. He reached over and pointed it out by laying his index finger lightly on the spot. She smiled and rubbed at the spot until it was gone.

"Thank you," she said. "I do not need to go to the city. I have no need of money, and I do not want to be famous."

"You're kidding, right? I mean, who doesn't want to be rich, or be famous?"

She looked at him with rounded, innocent eyes. "I do not want to be rich, and I do not want to be famous."

He had no response to that. She said it with such sincerity, he couldn't help but believe she meant it, but she was the first person he'd ever met who felt that way. He knew, though, that most people felt quite proprietary about their home towns—a feeling he didn't share, because he'd never really had a home town for longer than a year, not counting the orphanage—so, he avoided saying that anyone living in a one-horse town like Copper Cove should want anything that would take them away from it. Sure, the people were nice enough, with the exception of Cully Bryant and the old crazy man at the church, but there was so little to do. There was, in fact, nothing to do.

"Well have it your way," he said. "What are we having for dessert?"

She picked up the napkin again and held it in front of her face, peering at him over the top.

"What would you like to have for dessert?"

His breath caught in his throat. "Uh, I, uh—"

She frowned. "Do you not find me desirable?"

` "No, I mean, yes . . . of course, you're desirable, it's just—"

She stood and leaned in toward him. The shift ballooned out, revealing her conical breasts. He felt hot all over.

"If I am desirable," she whispered. "Why do you push me away?"

"I'm not pushing you away, it's just—"

"Then, you do want me?" He clenched his eyes shut. She was so close now he could feel the warmth of her breath on his face and smell the aroma of some flowery soap.

"I guess, I mean, I—"

She stopped him with her lips, pressing until his lips parted, and he felt her tongue slip inside his mouth. One part of him wanted to pull away, but the stirring in his loins pushed him forward. Then, he felt her hand, at first, lightly on his upper thigh, then higher and pressing harder, and whatever resistance he might have had melted like frost on a windshield when the defroster is set on high.

CHAPTER 24

The blaring of car horns and the 'whee-wha' sound of an ambulance siren yanked William Lewis from a sound sleep. One of the drawbacks of having a place so close to George Washington University Hospital was the frequency of ambulances carrying patients to the emergency room at all hours of day or night—but, especially at night. He winced as another horn blared, triggering a stabbing pain behind his eyelids. It had been another Saturday night of trying to see how long it would take to drink himself into oblivion or which of the staggering bimbos in whatever club he'd ended up in would end up in his bed. Slowly he opened his eyes and turned his head. The other half of his bed was empty, and there was no indentation in the pillow. The drink must have won. Though, from the way his head throbbed, it must have taken longer than it usually did, and he must have broken his record for number of drinks.

He eased out of bed. Even the creaking of the floor boards hurt his head. He made his way to the bathroom like a geriatric, bent over and cupping his hands to the sides of his head trying to squeeze the pain away-- unsuccessfully. After disrobing he entered the shower and turned the water on, first cold to wake up completely, and then as hot as he could stand it, letting it massage the back of his neck. After a few minutes, the ache in his head had subsided to a minor throbbing annoyance, about a six on the pain scale. He scrubbed until his body was as red as if he'd lain in the sun too long, but after drying off he finally decided that his hangover wasn't fatal. He brushed his teeth, but left off shaving. He didn't trust his still shaking hands with sharp objects, not even the tiny strips of metal in his shaver.

Back in the bedroom he pulled on a pair of grey chinos and a Baltimore Ravens tee shirt and slipped his bare feet into a pair of black loafers. It was Sunday, and as far as he was concerned, he was overdressed for what he planned to do, which was nothing.

He padded into the apartment's tiny kitchen where he put a mug of water in the microwave. He set it for two minutes, and while the machine whirred, he took a box of Cheerios and a bowl from the cabinet. He filled the bowl with the donut-shaped cereal, and then took a jar of roasted peanuts from the cabinet and dumped a handful of the nuts into the cereal. To this he added milk. Just then the microwave dinged, signaling that his water was hot. He took the mug out and spooned in a teaspoon of Taster's Choice instant coffee, stirring until the brown gunk had dissolved off the spoon.

Standing at the counter he alternated; a spoon of cereal, a sip of coffee. When cereal and coffee were half consumed, his brain kicked back into gear, and he remembered why he'd been unable to pick up any of the girls who were hanging on the bar at the club—he couldn't even remember its name— the night before. He'd been slumped at the bar, downing one drink after another and worrying about Bradley. His worry must have shown on his face. On most nights when he cruised the bars, he'd be approached by some young woman before he'd half finished his first drink. *Last night I must have looked like a real turnoff, or a pervert looking for someone to ravage.* Now that he was almost sober, his worry returned.

It was unlike Bradley to go out of town and not call to check in. The guy was anal retentive about such things. *If only I knew where he was and what he was doing. Shit, this is messing with my social life.*

He kept eating, drinking and worrying. By the time both cereal and coffee had been consumed, and he was contemplating a second cup of coffee, his cell phone rang and buzzed at the same time, making an awful racket on the granite top of the counter where he'd obviously tossed it at whatever ungodly hour he'd finally come home. He picked it up and looked at the screen. A 202 area code showed up, but no caller ID. He considered not answering, but something told him the call might be important. If it turned out to be a wrong number, or worse, a telemarketer who didn't care that they weren't supposed to call cell phones, he'd have some fun with them before giving them the verbal finger and hanging up.

"Hello," he said.

"Is this William Lewis?" a female voice said.

"Maybe, who are you?"

"This is Rebecca Davis, and I need to speak urgently with Mr. William Lewis."

"Oh, Professor Davis," he said. "Sorry, I didn't recognize your number. Yeah, this is Bill Lewis. What's up?"

"I was working on some papers in my office yesterday afternoon, when I got a call from that sheriff from Calvert County, Sheriff Baxter, remember him?"

"Yeah, he's the guy we talked to. What'd he have to say?"

There was a pause, and he could hear papers shuffling. "Oh, here it is," she said. "He said he tried calling you, but couldn't get through, so he called the number we called from, which happens to be my office number." He heard her clearing her throat.

"Anyway, he said he got curious about the case, so he called the Prince George's County Sheriff's Office and asked them to check. They got back to him yesterday morning. Apparently, Bradley stopped at a convenience store on the highway and made some small purchases and an ATM withdrawal. He was last seen heading south on Route 4, but there's no evidence that he arrived in Chesapeake Beach or any of the other towns along the bay."

He felt a chill in the small of his back. "What did the sheriff think might have happened?"

"That's just it," she said, and the concern in her voice was clear. "He has no idea. He said he checked for accident reports along that route, and there were none, nor have there been any admissions in any of the hospitals in his county. By the way, I tried calling you yesterday evening and last night, and couldn't get through either."

That, he knew, was because he always turned his phone off when he went out carousing. He hated having the damn thing ring right in the middle of a seduction. It was a major mood killer. "Oh, I guess I must have turned it off," he said. "I was busy and didn't want to be disturbed. I tried calling Bradley a dozen times yesterday, and kept getting that damned 'out of service area' message, so I just gave up."

"Yes," she said. "I tried as well, and got the

same thing." There was a pause. "I'm beginning to worry. Do you think something's happened to him?"

He wanted to say 'no,' because Bradley was a tough son of a bitch who could take care of himself, but he couldn't bring himself to lie. Tough he might be, but he never turned his phone off for such long periods. At the same time, he couldn't bring himself to say 'yes' either. Losing Lena was as traumatic for him as it had been for Bradley. She'd been like a sister. Bradley was like a brother. They were the only family he had, and if he lost them both he . . . he didn't even want to think about it.

"What are we going to do?" she asked. "He might be in some kind of trouble."

Her use of 'we' wasn't lost on him. For her own reasons she was as worried as he was. And, she'd asked a damn good question: what could they do? What would Bradley do if it was him in a similar situation?

"Are you up for a road trip?" he asked.

CHAPTER 25

Bradley woke up slowly at first, and then, when he remembered the events of the previous evening, he bolted upright in bed. He looked to his left. That side of the bed was empty, but the sheets were rumpled, and there was a dent in the pillow. Looking closely, he saw a couple of strands of dark hair in the indentation. He panicked.

Oh shit, I did it! I can't believe I went through with it. It wasn't supposed to happen. I wasn't supposed to do it. Oh, my God, what have I done?

He threw the blanket aside and swung his legs off the bed. He sat there, his shoulders slumped and his head in his hands.

After five minutes, during which time the only thing that moved was his chest in its in and out breathing, he finally sat up straight and took a deep breath. Nothing to do, he thought, but to face up to it like a man. He was sure he could make her understand. He was a man in mourning, distraught, and not thinking clearly. What happened, happened, but it must never happen again, because . . . well, he thought, just because.

He checked his watch on the nightstand. It was five past seven. Time for a quick shower before breakfast and time to think over what he would say when he saw her. He could still smell her scent on the sheets, and was momentarily aroused. He hurried into bathroom where he turned the shower on to full cold, stripped and stepped under the piercing cold spray. Looking down, he saw that the cold water had immediately had the desired effect, so he added hot water until he'd achieved a comfortable temperature, and tried scrubbing what he'd done off his body.

Cleaned and changed, he stripped the sheets off the bed and the pillowcases off the pillows and dumped them into a pile outside his door. He realized as he did so that he'd not seen a chambermaid or any other staff of the inn since his arrival. That would give him a subject to open the conversation with Stark.

When he arrived downstairs he was surprised not to see her in the lobby or the dining room. He was standing in the doorway looking confused, when she came in from the back door. She smiled when she saw him, and rushed over. She placed a hand on his chest.

"Good morning, Bradley. Did you sleep well?"

"I, ah, I slept okay . . . I think. Funny thing, though; I don't remember what time I went to sleep."

She smiled and tickled him under the chin. "Silly man, you were getting drowsy when I left, and that was around midnight. I imagine you must have fallen asleep before I was out of the room."

"You were there that late? Wow! I'm having trouble remembering anything that happened after we finished dinner."

When that thought hit him, he felt another cold stab in his lower back. He realized that from the moment her hand had gripped him things were a blur, like events seen through filmy gauze.

She caressed his cheek. "There is no need for you to remember," she said. "I can remember for the both of us."

Not sure just what she meant by that, he decided to change the subject so he could regain control of the conversation—if, in fact, he'd ever had control of it.

"I need the linens changed in my room. I sweat a lot in my sleep."

"You, my dear man, sweat a lot at other times too. Do not worry; I will see that your linens are changed right away."

"Uh, I was kind of hoping you'd join me for breakfast," he said. "I think there are some things we need to talk about."

"I have already eaten, but I will be back shortly and join you in a cup of coffee." Again she caressed his cheek and peered deeply into his eyes. "Would that be okay with you?"

As if he had a choice in the matter. This was more evidence that she was running the entire inn by herself, because if otherwise, it should only have been a few moments for her to locate the chambermaid and instruct her to change his room.

"Sure, that'll be fine," he said as she gently took his elbow and led him to what he was beginning to think of as his 'usual' table.

She got him seated and brought a tray with his breakfast, which consisted of a stack of four golden brown and fluffy pancakes, a rectangle of hash brown potatoes, fluffy yellow scrambled eggs, and two dark brown sausages. She poured a cup of coffee for him, set another cup on the table opposite him, winked and walked away.

Her behavior got stranger to Bradley with each passing minute, each new incident, but the aroma of the breakfast said hello to his empty stomach and, in the throes of that steamy love affair, all else was forgotten for the moment.

He'd cleaned his plate and had almost finished his coffee by the time she returned; just enough time, he thought, to change his linens and clean his room He wondered why she went to such lengths to conceal the fact that she had no other employees, and decided to ask her about it.

"Welcome back," he said. "You're just in time to join me as I have my second cup of coffee."

He poured a cup for her, then stood and pulled out the chair. She smiled and curtsied before taking the offered chair.

He refilled his own cup and then leaned forward with his elbows on the table; his chin propped on the backs of his overlapped hands and regarded her levelly. She took a sip of coffee, glancing at him over the rim of the cup.

"Did you enjoy your breakfast?" she asked as she put her cup down.

He continued to stare at her. "It was great. My compliments to the chef . . . you're one hell of a good cook."

Her eyes went wide and her brows arched upwards. "Me? W-what on earth do you mean?"

He reached over and laid a hand on hers.

"Come on, Eve," he said. "You and I both know that it's you who is doing the cooking here. In fact, I'll bet you just cleaned my room." She began shaking her head. "No, wait . . . look, I haven't been snooping around or anything, if that's what you're worried about, but it would be obvious to a blind man that there's no one else in this place."

She blushed. Her smile faded. She looked down at his hand over hers. Finally, she heaved a sigh and looked him in the eyes.

"You are right. I have no employees here. There is only me," she said in a quiet voice. "But, look around you. Do you see any other guests? If you had paid attention to the register when you signed in you would have seen that the last guest to check in was more than three years ago."

He patted her hand. "That's nothing to be ashamed of. Heck, the way the economy's been going the past few years, most people are lucky to have a roof over their heads. I admire you for being able to hang in all by yourself like you have."

Her expression was hopeful. "Then, you are not disappointed in me?"

"Of course not, why—, wait, why should you worry about what I think?"

She looked down. Bright spots of red blossomed on her cheeks.

"B-because you are . . . important to me."

His cheeks reddened, but not from embarrassment. This was moving too fast, and had gone too far.

"Look, Eve," he said. "We need to talk. I . . . don't remember what we did last night, but I have a feeling that I owe you an apology. I let things go farther than they should have gone."

"B-but, the things you said last night—"

"Look, for some reason . . . maybe I had too much wine . . . I don't remember what I said or what I did last night. I'm sorry, maybe I should check out and stay somewhere else if this is too uncomfortable for you, but you and me, well, there can't be a 'you and me.' Do you understand?"

A single tear leaked from her left eye and flowed slowly down her cheek. She reached up with her left hand and wiped it off before it reached her lips. When she looked at him, her eyes were dark, and her expression was smoldering. Bradley felt a chill all over his body.

"I am sorry, Bradley," she said. Her voice was hard. "But, that is not the way it works. Last night you and I were joined. Only death can break the bonds we forged."

Bradley snatched his hand away from hers and stared at her, his brows furrowed in anger.

"What the hell do you mean by that? Are you threatening me or something?"

"No, Bradley my dearest. I am merely informing you of the truth of the situation. By entering me last night, you bound your soul to mine. We are now one in the eyes of the master."

"The master? What are you talking about? Is this some kind of cult?"

"No, my dearest," she said. She smiled, but Bradley saw no mirth in her dark eyes. "We are not a cult, or at least, not as you understand a cult. We are a community; a very old community; and now, you are a part of that community."

All he could do was sit there, shaking his head. He heard her words, but nothing she'd just said made any sense.

"What in the bloody hell are you talking about? I'm not part of anything."

"But, you are, Bradley. Mating with me sealed that."

"Ma-, you call it . . . yeah, I guess that's better than calling it screwing," he said. Then, it hit him. Her strange language, his inability to remember the evening. "Hey, you put something in my drink, didn't you?"

Her smile answered his question.

"Why? Why would you do a thing like that?" he asked. "Hell, you could have just asked."

"I do not think so, Bradley," she said. "You are not like the others, who would have done what I asked, just because I asked. Your sense of loyalty to your dead wife held you back. I did what I had to do to fulfill the master's orders."

He was getting steamed now.

"Who the fuck is this 'master' you keep talking about?"

"You will find out tonight, Bradley," she said. "When we hold the welcoming ceremony."

"I don't think so." He rose. "I'm getting the hell out of here right now."

"And, where will you go. Your vehicle does not work, and it is too far to walk to the highway, even if he would allow you to leave .

. . which he will not, by the way."

"What's he gonna do, shoot me?"

"Oh, Bradley, you are so quaint." She laughed her mirthless laugh again. The naïve looking woman who'd greeted him when he first arrived in Copper Cove was gone now. He didn't recognize the woman sitting across from him. "He has no need to shoot you. Your body and mind belong to him now. Once our bodies were linked together, he entered your mind, and now he controls you."

He shook himself and clenched his eyes shut.

"Lady, you're totally bat shit, you know that."

"There is no need for such vulgarity, my darling. If you do not believe me, get up and leave . . . right now."

He shoved the chair back and stood. She eyed him like a hawk watching an unsuspecting rabbit in the grass, with hooded lids and a half smile on her face. He walked toward the dining room door, crossed into the lobby and headed for the exit. When he arrived at the double exit doors, his feet stopped moving. It was as if they were super-glued to the floor. He started to life his hand to push the door, but could not will it to move.

"Turn around, Bradley." Her voice came from behind him. Slowly he turned to face her. "You need have no fear. You can move about the inn freely, but you must have me at your side if you wish to leave the building."

She walked up to him and laid a hand on his cheek. Salty tears of frustration coursed over his brown cheeks. He wanted to punch her face, but when the thought appeared, his arms again froze at his sides.

Leaning in close, she whispered in his ears, "Do not worry, my pet. You are confused now, as is to be expected. But, in time, you will come to accept it, and perhaps even like it. Now, go to your room and wait for me. I have preparations to make. This will be a big evening for Copper Cove. We have waited far too long already."

His legs started moving as of their own volition, toward the stairs. His mind, screaming silently inside his head, seemed to be the only thing that remained his. As he approached the stairs, he heard her mutter, "He will be most pleased, most pleased indeed."

CHAPTER 26

It had taken William the better part of the morning to get his hangover under sufficient control for sitting cooped up in a car for hours. Davis picked him up at 11:30. They'd argued over the phone about which car to take, and she'd finally convinced him that his little MG two-seater was impractical, so they took her Volvo S-60.

They stopped at the convenience store in Upper Marlboro and talked to the Pakistani man who operated it. After they described Bradley, he told them he vaguely recalled him; mainly that he'd bought snacks and paid mostly in coins. He confirmed what the sheriff had told Davis; that Bradley had driven south when he left the store.

For the first few minutes after leaving the store, they rode in silence, Davis concentrating on the highway and Lewis staring morosely out the window at the passing scenery.

Finally, after they'd passed a rundown trailer park and there was nothing on either side of the highway to see but trees and no other traffic around them, Davis turned her head slightly to the right, enabling her to see Lewis slumped in his seat, and still see the road.

"So, tell me how you and Bradley met," she said, breaking the silence.

He scrunched up further in his seat and turned to look back at her.

"He never told you?"

'Uh, well, if you must know, Bradley and I never talked much, other than about department business. Other than that time he and his wife had the party for the faculty, I'd never really encountered him in a social setting."

"Yeah, that's Brad right enough," he said. "If it hadn't been for Lena he probably wouldn't have known anyone else besides me." He leaned back and closed his eyes for a second, then snapped them open. "We met, the three of us, at freshman orientation." He then went on to explain how Bradley, Lena and he had been gawky teens, orphans all, they'd spent their lives in foster homes or orphanages and were ill at ease around their self-assured classmates, so they'd hung back from the others. With everyone else in the pack of over two hundred incoming freshmen abuzz at the prospect of meeting new people, the three loners found themselves slowly pushed into each other's orbits. Lena had taken the initiative of introducing herself, first to Bradley and then to William, and eventually they'd drifted into a corner, ignored by everyone else, where they formed the basis of what became a deep trilateral friendship.

"So, being orphans, the three of you sort of drifted together," she said. "I can see that. I imagine the first year of college was somewhat traumatic for each of you."

"Actually, it wasn't," William said. "You know, for most kids it is because it's the first time they're away from home on their own. For us, though, it was just another foster home. We had no family to miss, and we'd already experienced so many changes in environment as we were moved from foster home to foster home, there wasn't anything intimidating about it."

"I'm surprised, then, that the three of you didn't establish leadership of your peers. You could have guided them through the trauma of separation from family."

He laughed harshly. "You'd think so, but you'd be wrong," he said. "You have to remember, the three of us had no real sense of family, and we'd learned to be wary of strangers. Here we were in a room full of strangers, so our default position was to remain uninvolved. The surprising thing is that we drifted toward each other. I don't know, maybe it was a recognition of our similar backgrounds. Whatever, we became friends that day, and remain so."

Davis turned her attention back to the road, and began drumming her long fingers on the steering wheel. After a while, she looked back at Lewis.

"I think I understand things better now. The three of you became like a single organism. I imagine each of you brought something unique to the relationship. Now, however, with a part of the organism missing, the remaining two feel set adrift, and each of you is finding your own unique way to cope. I suspect that with you it's the hedonistic pursuit of pleasure. Other than maybe seeking solitude, I'm not sure what it is with Bradley."

"Brad's a hard person to get to know," William said. "Before he became friends with me and Lena, he'd been pretty much a loner. But, I can tell you this; as a friend he's aces, and he's got this thing about loyalty. If you're his friend, he'll do anything for you."

Davis made a 'hm' noise, but didn't otherwise respond. William lounged back in the seat and turned his attention back to the scenery, but quickly became bored by mile after mile of nothing but trees. The green tableau was finally broken by a narrow, two-lane road on the right that slashed through a field of high grass. He glimpsed the sign as they sped past, a thick wooden board with faded lettering that said, 'Copper Cove, est.

1668 – 12 miles.'

"Hey, did you see that?" he asked.

"See what?"

"That road back there. There was a sign, apparently there's a little town back in the woods."

"Sorry," she said. "I had my eyes on the road. Of course, that's no surprise. This part of Maryland has a lot of little farming communities."

"Yeah, but the sign said this one was established over 300 years ago."

Her right brow arched upwards. "Really?"

"Yeah, really. Bradley was always interested in history. I wonder if he might have gone there to check it out."

"You have a smart phone, right? Why don't you look it up?"

Of course, he thought. I would have thought of that eventually. He pulled his phone from his jacket pocket, saw that he had a strong signal, and logged onto the Internet. He pulled up the Yahoo search engine and typed in the words, 'Copper Cove, MD.' Several pages showed, but the only ones for 'Copper Cove' in Maryland were for a chain of restaurants. There were towns in Arizona and Mexico called Copper Cove, but none in Maryland.

"According to Yahoo there's no such place in Maryland," he said.

"Why don't you try Google," she suggested.

Google gave him the same results he'd

already gotten on Yahoo. "Nope, same thing . . . there's no such place."

She eased off on the gas, dropping the car's speed from 70 to 50, and looked askance at him.

"That's impossible. I mean, if there's sign, it means the town was once there, so there should be an entry. *Everything's* on the Internet. Unless, of course, the sign's someone's idea of a joke."

"That's not . . . well, I guess . . . no, that sign looked *old*, I mean *real* old. I can't see anyone going to that length for a joke."

"So, what are you saying?"

"Call it a gut feeling," he said. "But, I'm willing to bet money Brad saw that sign and turned down that road to explore it. It's probably an old ghost town, and maybe the trees are so thick it blocks phone signals, or there are no towers around."

"What are you saying . . . you want to check it out?"

He shrugged. "Well, if you don't mind."

She leaned forward and looked up at the sky through the windshield.

"Okay, but it's getting late in the day," she said. "If it turns out to be a ghost town, we'll be getting to Chesapeake Beach after dark."

"Thanks. It's only 12 miles from the highway according to the sign. We ought to be able to get there, look around, and be back out here in no more than half an hour."

She'd checked the rearview mirror to make

sure there were no cars behind her and started spinning the wheel for a U-turn before the words were out of his mouth.

Charles Ray

CHAPTER 27

Bradley spent the rest of the day in his room. He tried reading, but his mind kept wandering, so he tossed the book on top of his duffle bag and lay back on top of the bed covering, and promptly fell asleep. But, his sleep was troubled by the same thoughts that had interfered with his reading, only, in his dreams the thoughts were weirder. He found himself alone in a . . . space . . . surrounded by a roiling grey mist that seemed to close in on him, squeezing him until he could hardly breathe. The more he tried pulling away, the more the mist squeezed him. He opened his mouth to protest . . . to scream . . . but, no sound came out. Then, he heard a sound. It seemed to be coming from a long way off, a rapping sound, like a woodpecker. He tried turning his head, but the mist held him firm.

"Bradley, Bradley," a voice said. He tried reaching for the voice.

He felt a pressure on his chest.

The voice came again, "Bradley, Bradley, wake up."

He had troubling focusing his eyes. A shadowy figure loomed over him. "Hm, what?" he said.

"Bradley, wake up. It is time. We must not keep him waiting."

Eve Stark's voice slowly cleared and became recognizable. The shadowy figure morphed into her, standing over his bed with a hand on his chest, gently shaking him.

He remembered the scene in the dining room and suddenly felt cold. Shoving her hand away, he sat up and rubbed at his eyes. "W-what did you do to me? Did you put something in my food?"

She recoiled from him with a stricken look on her face.

"No, I put nothing in your food, and for the record, I did not administer drugs to you last night."

"Then, why am I having trouble remembering things?" He glared at her. "Why can't I walk out the front door? Explain that, why don't you."

She reached for him, but he shrank back from her.

"I . . . I am so sorry that you are upset, Bradley," she said. "It is not me doing this to you, it is . . . him . . . he has chosen you."

He looked confused.

"He . . . who the hell is he, and what do

you mean, has chosen me?"

She reached out to him again. "Please, Bradley, get up and get dressed, and come downstairs with me. I promise you that all will be explained."

He eyed her with a mixture of suspicion and anger. Finally, he shrugged. He would certainly get no answers to the mystery sitting on his bed sulking. Slowly, he stood. As she reached out to him, he pushed her hand away and went into the bathroom. He took his time washing his face and brushing his teeth. When he returned to the bedroom, she was sitting on the chair in the corner looking forlorn.

"Okay, let's get this over with," he said. "I need some answers."

She stood and walked to the door, looking over her shoulder, but he coldly returned her hopeful gaze. They were silent for the rest of the journey to the dining room.

When Bradley walked into the dining room he stopped, stunned by what he saw.

The tables had been shoved to the sides of the room, and what looked like it might be the entire population of the town waited in the center. All eyes were on the entrance. Except for Cully Bryant, who stood in front of the crowd with a sullen look, everyone was smiling. Bradley walked in until he and Eve were ten feet from the group and then he stopped, not of his own volition, but as if someone had placed a hand on his chest.

Along with Bryant, Bradley recognized Jason Warfield, Philo, the mechanic, and Esmerelda, the woman from the gift shop. They smiled warmly at him.

"Well, ladies and gentlemen," Eve said. "Our guest of honor has arrived."

There was a smattering of applause and murmurs of welcome, again with the exception of Bryant, who continued to frown. This wasn't lost on Eve who walked over and planted herself directly in front of the scowling man.

"Cully, as mayor of our little town, I think it would be nice if you gave Bradley a formal welcome, do you not agree?" There was steel in her voice.

Bryant held his hands up in a defensive gesture and took a step backwards. "Would it not be better, Eve, if you did that?"

"No, Cully, it should be *you. He* desires that it be so."

Bryant's face went pale and his lips trembled.

"Uh, okay, if I must," he said. He stepped forward and made a half turn, his right side to Bradley. "We, the citizens of Copper Cove would like to welcome you, Bradley Matthews, to our community. Henceforth, you are as one of us, and we are one with you."

Bradley couldn't turn his head, but he was able to move his eyes until he could see Eve. She had a look of satisfaction on her face.

"What does this mean?" he asked. He was surprised that he was able to think and speak. Apparently, whatever she'd—or this mysterious 'he'—done to him only extended to his large motor functions. "What does he mean I'm now one of you?"

The woman, Esmerelda, stepped forward. "Eve, mayhap I can explain things for Bradley?"

Eve bowed. "Of course, Esmerelda," she said. "As the elder matron of the community, it is appropriate that you perform that duty."

She didn't look like an elder matron as she stepped forward, the shy smile on her elfin face and the curvy body beneath the tight fitting sheath she wore gave her the appearance of a precocious teenager. She moved to stand in front of Bradley, smiling coquettishly up at him and fluttering her lashes.

"Copper Cove was established in 1668 by a group of a hundred settlers who had come to this area from the Old World," she began, sounding like a student reciting a lesson learned by rote. "Unlike other settlers, though, this group was not solely English. Of the original settlers, there were English, who were actually in the minority, Welsh, and Irish. What bound them together, and caused them to establish a settlement away from others, was their mutual belief in the *fae,* the spirits they had left behind as they fled persecution in the old country. One of the settlers, an adventurous man by the name of Seamus O'Hare, found this place during one of his hunting trips, and he discovered that a new world *fae* occupied the area. He went back to his settlement, a small one near the headwaters of the bay, and brought back others who, like him, believed in the spirits, and who chafed under the strict religious rules of the leaders of their settlements."

She fairly danced as she recited, her face glowing and her expression animated.

"The *fae* of this place was . . . is . . . a powerful spirit, more powerful than any they had ever encountered, and over time, they learned his story, and became one with him. His name is Ahnok, and he now welcomes you to become one with him."

She went on to describe Ahnok and the treachery he'd suffered at the hands of his duplicitous siblings, and how, over the centuries he'd developed a symbiotic relationship with the inhabitants of the town that had come to be known as Copper Cove.

"So, this Ahnok character . . . whatever he or it is," Bradley said when she stopped talking. "You're telling me he has control over you people?"

Eve stepped forward and put a hand on his arm.

"It is not quite like that," she said firmly. "Ahnok does not . . . control us. We have a special relationship with him."

Tactfully, Bradley removed her hand and

turned to her. "Was he controlling me this afternoon?"

"Uh . . . well, yes, but that was to keep you from leaving."

He glared at her. She took a step backwards, her eyes round with fright.

"Does he also keep *you* and any of the others from leaving?"

Jason Warfield stepped away from the group, smiling at Bradley.

"It is not like that, Bradley," he said. "I can leave town whenever I wish, and so can Philo."

"The rest of us have no reason to leave," Esmerelda said. "We have everything we want here in Copper Cove."

"Ahnok sees to that," Eve added.

"Maybe you have all that you need," Bradley said through clenched teeth. "But, I don't. I have no desire to stay in this place one minute longer." He sought Philo and fixed him with an icy stare. "I want my car fixed today, and I don't care what you have to do to get that done. I don't plan on waking up in your fair town tomorrow morning."

"I, I don't think I'm gonna be able to do that, Bradley," Philo said. He refused to make eye contact.

"I say let him go," Bryant said. "We do not need him here."

Eve whirled and pointed a finger at Bryant.

"That is not for you to say, Cully," she said. "It has been decided. Ahnok has informed me that he is the chosen one. He must stay."

"Whoa, just hold up there," Bradley said. "Don't I get a say in this?"

"Bradley, you do not understand what an honor it is to be chosen by Ahnok," Eve said. "There are many who would do anything to be in your place."

He pointed at Bryant. "You mean like old Cully, here? He seems like he's aching to be chosen, whatever the hell that means. I'm perfectly happy to step aside and let him take my place."

He moved toward the frowning man, surprised that whatever force that had been controlling him seemed to have slackened. He had no illusions, though, that if he made a break for the door that it would come back.

Bryant's mouth turned down in a sneer. "See, it is like I said. He is not worthy. We should let him go."

Bradley knew that the man was not speaking out of any feeling of goodwill toward him, but hoped the others—Eve Stark, in particular—would listen. Stark pushed forward, her face red with anger, and dashed that hope.

"Silence, Cully." Bryant's face paled and he took a step backwards. "It is not up to us. Ahnok has decided and thus it shall be."

She turned to face Bradley, her face still flushed, but her expression softened.

"Bradley, please at least listen to what we offer you." She stopped and her expression went blank for a few seconds. "No, listen to Ahnok. Let him tell you what lies ahead for you."

"What do you mean, listen to Ahnok?"

"Come with us to the lake. Ahnok wishes to speak to you directly."

Something about the way she said it set of warning bells in Bradley's mind. He remembered what the old man had said about staying away from the lake.

"Why do I have to go to the lake? If this Ahnok is so powerful that he can control my movements, why can't he come here and talk to me?"

"While Ahnok can project his thoughts and will to a distance, his spiritual form cannot cross water," Eve said. "He requires a physical form for that, and even then, he cannot come into contact with water."

"What happens when he comes into contact with water?"

Her brows bunched together and she frowned. Bradley felt a wave of cold pass through his body.

"It would destroy him," she said finally.

"Wait a minute, you mean this . . . whatever he is, can control you, but he can't go in the water?"

Eve opened her mouth to answer, but no sound came out. She got a glassy-eyed look on her face and her lips trembled. Everyone else in the room stood frozen in place like so many statues. Bradley was able to move his head a fraction to either side, but he couldn't get his arms or legs to move, and he felt cold all over. Finally, Stark blinked and turned to him.

:"Ahnok says that you are a strong human, and he wants to speak with you," she said. Her face was ashen and her lips still trembled.

"He apparently speaks to you, why doesn't he just do the same for me?"

"You do not understand. He wants to speak directly to you, he wishes to meet with you face-to-face. You must go across the lake to the island where he abides."

There was a collective gasp from several of the others.

"No one has ever done that," Bryant said.

"He has never sensed a worth vessel before. But, it is to be done now," Eve responded. "Ahnok has decreed it."

Bradley weighed his options. He wasn't buying this story about some mythical being living in the middle of the lake, able to control movements and thought. He was still puzzled at his inability to move earlier, and there was the old man and his warnings about the lake, but his rational mind told him that there was a simple explanation for what was going on. This was obviously some kind of cult. And, it was clear that Eve Stark was its leader. Through a combination of drugs, mind control, and sheer force of will, she seemed to be controlling things, like that nut, Jim Jones back in the 1970s. Bradley had read about him in one of the abnormal psychology classes he'd taken. The man had convinced several hundred people to commit suicide by drinking poison. He had no doubt that Stark was capable of something just as insane. After all, she'd played the naïve country maiden until she saw her chance. Then, she'd drugged and seduced him, and was now feeding him this bullshit line about some powerful spirit desiring him to stay—he tried not to imagine for what purpose. There was, of course, the incident in the hotel lobby when he'd been unable to move his feet. It was possible that she had some kind of drug, which she'd put in his food or wine, or both, that enable her to plant suggestions in his mind so that at certain times he wouldn't be able to control his muscle movements. He didn't know a lot about drugs, but, like any college student, he was aware of date rape drugs like Rohypnol that made victims compliant and erased memories—maybe she had some form of that which enabled auto-suggestion. That he was able still to think was a kind of proof of that. While he didn't fancy being in a small boat on the lake at night, or wandering around some weed-choked, snake-infested island in its middle, as he looked around the room, he assessed his chances. He had to get the hell out of Copper Cove, and his chances against this room full of people were about as good as a snowball rolling through hell without losing weight. Alone in a boat, or even on this island, with Stark, it was just possible that he could catch her off guard and escape. It was worth a shot. One thing for sure, he'd had enough of Copper Cove, and even if he had to walk, he was leaving.

"How am I supposed to do that?" he asked.

"Ahnok says that a vessel, a boat, will be at the shore of the lake," she said. "I am to accompany you to the island that sits in the middle of the lake. Once we arrive there, Ahnok will explain all to you."

As he'd expected. The two of them would be alone. Maybe he could overpower her and row the boat to the opposite side of the lake in the dark. He could hide in the woods. The thought of being in the woods after dark sent shudders down his spine, but even that would be preferable to another night in looneyville.

"Okay then, let's do it," he said.

CHAPTER 28

They hit the fog after only four miles. A thick, roiling blanket of greyish white mist, that made it impossible to see more than a few feet in front of the vehicle, surrounded them. William Lewis had been attempting to usc his smart phonc as a navigation device, but when they entered the fog, the device went blank.

"Damn," he said. "We must be in a skip zone. I don't have a signal."

Rebecca Davis, her hands gripping the steering wheel so tightly her knuckles were as white as ivory, was peering intently through the windshield and hoping they wouldn't come upon a deer or stray cow in the fog. She'd dropped her speed to 30 mph.

"Hm, that's not so unusual out here in

these one-horse towns," she said. "Contrary to the advertising, we have lots of places, even back in DC, that have no cell coverage."

"Yeah, I guess you're right. Maybe we'll get coverage when we get to this town."

"I certainly hope so," she said. "And, I hope this damned fog clears up. I can barely see the road."

There was little to say to that. William agreed with her. He hadn't seen fog so thick before, but the strangest thing about it was they never seemed to drive entirely *into* it; it was more like a bowl of fog had descended around their car and moved along with it. He shook himself, thinking that this was crazy.

After a few minutes of driving, maybe a total four miles, they came out of the fog. Literally, it just stopped. It was like driving through a curtain. The mist around them just disappeared, causing both to blink. William looked over his shoulder, but there behind them, receding into the distance as Davis picked up speed, was the curtain of white they'd driven through, stretching across the road and enveloping the trees on both sides. He shook his head and turned back to view the road ahead.

"Did you see that?" he asked.

"Yes, I did, and no, I don't get it either," she responded. "I'm just glad we're not driving through it anymore."

Outside the car, everything suddenly looked so normal, to William it looked abnormal. The perpetual grey had been replaced by a bright blue, cloudless sky above them, and deep green forest to the sides of the road, a razor straight ribbon of grey that slashed through the quiet countryside. By the time they'd gone ten miles from the highway, the bright blue sky had darkened. William didn't point that out, not wanting to hear Davis complain about being in the backwoods after dark.

As suddenly as the fog disappeared, the town appeared. It looked like most of the other small, rural Maryland towns he'd seen, and certainly not like a ghost town. The streets were clean and the buildings, while old, seemed to be well maintained. The road they drove on cut straight through and there didn't appear to be any appreciable cross streets. The only thing missing, he thought, was people. The streets and sidewalks were empty, giving him a creepy feeling. Before he had a chance to panic, he saw a group of people off to the left, moving between two buildings.

"Over there," he said. "There's a bunch of people, maybe we can ask them if they saw Brad."

Davis sped up, turning the wheel to park on that side of the street. William craned his neck to see where the group was going. Then, he saw a tall figure at the head of the group. Even in the fading light in the shadows between the buildings, Bradley was unmistakable. He would have been hard to miss anyway; a tall, dark man being followed—albeit slowly and seemingly unthreatening—by a group of white people.

"Damn," he said. "It's Brad over there with that bunch of people. I wonder what the hell's going on."

Davis peered through the window, but the front of the group was out of sight between the buildings.

"Are you sure?" she asked. "I see a bunch of people, but I don't see him."

"He was in front. He's out of sight now." He reached across and pressed the horn.

Davis jerked backwards at the blaring sound, and slapped his hand away.

"Stop that. You frightened me."

"Hell, it didn't work anyway." No one in the crowd seemed to pay any attention to the sound of the horn. "I can't believe nobody noticed a horn blowing. It's not like we're in the city or something where there's noise all the time."

Davis pulled into the curb and put the car in 'park.' "Okay, what do we do now, Sherlock?"

"Why, we follow them, of course."

"We can't drive through there. That alley's too narrow."

"We walk."

She gave him a wide-eyed look.

"We're a couple of strangers, in a strange town. Are you sure it's a good idea to go trailing after a mob of locals?"

"Aw, come on, Rebecca," he said. "This isn't Deliverance. Besides, I saw women in that crowd, so I'd hardly call it a mob."

Her look was skeptical. "Okay, but if that crowd turns hostile, don't get in front of me."

"Wha-, why?"

"Because I'm running right over you."

"You don't think you'd be able to outrun an angry mob, do you?"

"Don't have to. All I have to be able to do is outrun you."

Charles Ray

CHAPTER 29

After Bradley agreed to accompany them to the lake, the mood in the room lightened—except for Cully Bryant who continued to sulk and look angrily at him out of the corner of his eye.

Eve took his arm and the two of them led the group out of the inn and diagonally across the street in the direction of the old church. The townspeople were strung out behind them, walking quietly in their wake like a funeral procession. Considering their destination, he found that image appropriate.

As the church appeared in the distance, Eve steered him to the left toward a dark line of trees. A domelike shape, greyish white in color, could be seen protruding slightly above the tops of the trees. They were about halfway to the trees when he heard a car horn honk from behind them, but Eve kept pressure on his arm and continued to guide him onward.

When they were closer to the trees, Bradley was able to see that the mist wasn't behind them but hovering in the middle of a small lake instead. The lake, and he knew this must be Devil's Lake that he'd been warned against, was a rough oval about a quarter mile across at the widest and just under that on the other dimension. Even in the dim light, he could see the tangled skeletons of small trees and grass along the shore. He could only imagine what manner of creatures lived in that mass of rotting vegetation, and he wasn't anxious to find out.

A rowboat, its sides weather-beaten and peeling, was on the shore, half-in, half-out of the murky looking water, with two oars tilting up at the sides.

The crowd came to a halt about ten feet from the boat. Eve kept moving forward, with Bradley in her wake as if tethered to her. The front, bow, Bradley remembered for some reason, was on the bank of the lake. The rear end, which he remembered was aft or stern, bobbed gently up and down in rhythm with the movement of the lake's surface.

When they reached the boat, she released her hold on him and stepped daintily into the boat, holding onto the sides as she made her way to the stern. Once there, she turned and sat on the crosspiece that spanned from one side to the other and looked up at him. She pointed at the center of the boat.

"Please get in and take the oars, Bradley," she said. "You will want to push the vessel into the water a bit before getting in." Her tone wasn't harsh, but it was commanding.

He moved forward and grasped the pointed front end of the boat and started pushing it into the water, a task made easier by the main mass already being afloat. When the forward-most part was clear of the black muck of the lake shore, he stepped nimbly over the side and with his arms outspread to maintain his balance as the craft rocked from side to side, took the two steps that put him at the center crosspiece over which hung the oars. He sat facing her and placed his hands on the oars.

"Now, what do I do?" he asked. "I've never rowed a boat before."

She patiently explained how he should use one oar to turn the boat around, and when he had the bow pointed toward the center of the lake, how to use both oars to propel it forward—backwards for him—making slight course alterations by rowing more or less on one side than the other.

He very quickly had the craft sliding over the water. The only sounds were the creak of the wooden oars in the metal hooks set into the sides of the boat, the slap of the lake surface against the boat, her occasional quiet instructions to change course, and the call of some night bird in the distance.

The crowd on the shore of the lake got

smaller the farther out into the lake Bradley rowed. They just stood there in a loose grouping staring out over the water. Just before they were too far away to make out any details, Bradley saw two people approach the assembled group from the direction of town. It looked like a man and a woman, but it was too far away for him to be sure, and then he was too far away to see more than tiny, doll-like figures forming into a larger, even more indistinct mass.

"We are nearing the island," Eve said. "Keep a little to your left."

A few seconds later, he heard a scraping and squishing sound and felt a jolt as the bow of the boat hit something. He looked over his shoulder and saw a thick stand of gnarled and twisted vegetation. At the sides he saw the rotten looking sea grass, black mud, and dark water lapping the mud. When he dipped the oars, they immediately struck the mud only a few inches below the surface.

He stood, got out and pulled the boat up onto the shore so that Eve could step out.

"Okay, boss lady," he said. "Where do we go from here?"

She pointed over his shoulder. Turning, all he saw was what appeared to be an impenetrable, dark thicket, with tendrils of wispy, grey fog swirling in and around the gnarled foliage.

"Ahnok is just beyond here, in the center of the island," she said.

"You're kidding, right? You expect me to go in there." He pointed at the thicket. "Who the hell knows what kind of snakes or other dangerous animals might be in there?"

She smiled at him and laid a hand on his arm. "Now, now, Bradley, except for a few northern copperheads and timber rattlesnakes, Maryland has no dangerous snakes."

"Oh, only two," he said. "That's exactly two too many for me."

"There is nothing to worry about. Neither of those two are on the island, and even if they were, Ahnok will protect you."

He made a snorting sound. She was taking this spirit thing too far. He wasn't about to walk into a possibly snake-infested thicket to humor her.

"Okay, enough is enough, Eve. I am not going into that thicket. There is no Ahnok. I know you're running some kind of cult, and I've played along, but I'm not moving another step until you admit what you're up to, and then we can get back across the lake so I can get the hell out of this town."

A sad look crossed her face. "And, tell me, Bradley," she said. "Just what do you think is going on here?"

The anger that had been simmering below the surface erupted.

"What do I think's going on?" His voice rose in pitch in volume. "I think you've been drugging me, for one thing. And, another thing, and I'm sorry to be saying this, but I think you and the rest of the people in this town are bat shit crazy."

"Poor, poor, Bradley," she said. "You do not understand what is happening. I assure you that I have not drugged you, and as for your belief that we are crazy, well—" She stopped suddenly and her face went slack. She stood like that for several seconds. Then, she shook herself, blinked and looked stonily at Bradley. "Ahnok says that he *will* bond with you, so he will give you a demonstration of his power. Do not try to resist, please."

"Wha—" Before Bradley could finish, he felt his left foot move forward. This was followed by the right foot, and then, like a clumsily manipulated puppet, he found himself plunging through the thicket. Branches whipped at his face, and he bumped into a small tree, bruising his nose, then backed away, turned awkwardly and made his way around the tree and move deeper into the bushes. He imagined seeing himself and almost laughed. *Damn, why can I think freely like this, but can't control my own body?* He twisted his head around and saw Eve following close behind him, a concerned look on her face.

The thicket ended suddenly, and he found himself, panting from the trek, standing beside Eve in a circular clearing. In the center of the clearing stood a cylindrical black stone about three feet in height and ten inches across. The mist swirled near, but never touched the stone. Bradley felt a chilly feeling all over his body, and, without knowing how he knew, was aware that it emanated from the stone.

"What the bloody hell!"

"Welcome, Bradley Matthews." The voice was deep and commanding, and echoed inside his skull.

He turned to Eve, a question in his eyes.

"Yes, Bradley, I heard him," she said. "That is the voice of Ahnok."

Belief didn't come easy. Bradley Matthews viewed himself as a rational man, a person who needed proof of a thing to accept it. He was getting that proof, but his mind still rebelled.

"What does he want with me?"

"Why do you not ask him yourself?"

Shrugging, Bradley turned and faced the stone. He felt a bit foolish talking to an inert rock, but decided to humor her.

"Okay, Ahnok," he said. "What do you want from me?"

"It is very simple, Bradley Matthews. I wish to become one with you so that I might once again walk upon the earth and feel it beneath my feet, that I might feel the wind upon my face, and gaze upon the blue sky."

The voice washed over him like a strong wind, and it clearly came from, or certainly seemed to come from, the stone. It took

Bradley a few seconds to regain his composure.

"I don't understand. How would you do that, and why, and more importantly, why me?"

"Sit my child, and I will explain it to you."

Bradley felt a loosening of the control over his limbs, and a prickling sensation in his head.

"You are indeed a strong one," the voice of Ahnok said. *"I find it difficult to control your body, and almost impossible to control your mind. I have indeed chosen well."*

None of what the disembodied voice was saying made sense, but Bradley's curiosity was aroused. He found a relatively dry spot in front of the stone and sat cross-legged, his hands resting on his knees.

"Okay, I'm ready to hear what you have to say."

Ahnok's voice began, slowly at first and gradually increasing tempo, spinning his tale.

He and his kind, he said, had existed in this place for eons before there were any humans walking the land. They'd had corporeal existence, and had had the land to themselves, sharing it only with the beasts and birds that roamed unmolested, preying only upon each other insofar as was needed for sustenance. Ahnok and his brethren (and sisters) had no need to feed upon them, for they took their own sustenance from the energy of the surroundings; the land, air and water.

Then, the first human, mortals, came. The dusky skinned natives made their way from the direction of the setting sun. The first ones to arrive were by any measure primitive, living in huts made from whatever loose material they could find, and eating nuts and berries and what small animals they could trap in the snares they made from vines and twigs. As time passed their social institutions became more sophisticated and their communities larger.

Ahnok and his kin mostly ignored them at first, dipping into the minds of a few on occasion, but as their communities grew, curiosity overcame reticence and they began making limited contact with greater numbers. It had only been mildly interesting, giving rise to many legends among the humans who were vaguely aware of the immortal intrusions, which gave rise to many legends of spirits, such as Wendigo, the man-eating spirit. But, when the different groups started making war on each other, the interest of some of Ahnok's kindred increased, for they had never known war or conflict.

When the strange humans with the pale skin and different colored hair arrived and began their campaign of exterminating the first arrivals with strange weapons that spit fire and smoke and killed from greater distances than the pointed sticks in use up until that time, the level of interest rose even higher. Some among them, Ahnok said, became addicted to the excitement they felt from the violent actions of humans at war.

This led eventually to conflict among themselves, in particular a small group that Ahnok called his bloodthirsty brothers and treacherous sister, whose names he refused to utter. The culmination of their conflict, and the ultimate treachery, Ahnok said in what sounded to Bradley like a whining voice, was his siblings ganging up on him, separating him from his corporeal form, and exiling him on this ball of mud in the middle of a lake which he could not traverse, thus imprisoning him.

"And, here I have been for some three hundred of your human years," Ahnok said. *"Cut off from the world and contact with you most interesting creatures."*

"But, you're able to control humans even from here on the island," Bradley said.

"Alas, only to a limited degree, and my range is limited. If I had a corporeal form, my power would be greatly enhanced."

Bradley's mind latched onto Ahnok's last sentence, and he didn't like the thought that it evoked.

"What do you want from me?" He felt foolish standing there talking to a rock and a voice in the air, but the sight of Eve out of the corner of his eye, cowering as she focused on the ground at her feet, told him that it was real, whatever it was. It couldn't be happening, but it was. "Why am I here?" he asked.

"You are here, Bradley Matthews, because I need you. You are strong, from a strong people. You are not the first of your kind that I have seen. Before I was imprisoned, people like you were brought to this land. I was immediately drawn to them. Like the first humans, they were close to nature, but they were made of stronger stuff. When the pale ones, who called themselves Europeans and all manner of other sub-names, came, it was soon clear that they would overwhelm the original inhabitants, who they called Indians for some strange reason. I would have, at the time, preferred dealing with these new people, these Nubians from a place called Africa, but they were treated as property, not much better than the four-legged beasts they used to till their fields. I would have been too constrained, so I avoided them. From the three who are allowed to leave this area for short periods, Jason, Philo, and Curry, I have learned that your people are no longer indentured. You would make the perfect vessel for me."

"What do you mean, vessel?"

"As I know Eve has told you, I am unable to cross water in my present form. By occupying your body, I will be able to leave this island and cross the water. I can again be free."

"Uh, it's been weird having you control my movements from outside," Bradley said. "And, it's a little strange standing here talking to a . . . stone. I'm not sure I want you inside my body."

The entity, Ahnok, didn't reply right away. The silence hung heavy in the air. Even the crickets and night birds were silent.

Finally, the voice came again, *"I can understand your reluctance. You are a fiercely independent being. I ask but temporary shelter within your body to enable me to cross the water. Once I am off the island, I will leave you and find other suitable . . . accommodations."*

Bradley knew he'd just been lied to. Ordinarily one needs verbal clues to detect evasion and lying, but something in the words, tone, or just the fact that Ahnok had hesitated before speaking, told Bradley that this . . . thing was trying to run a number on him. But, he also knew that he was in something of a bind. He was here on this island, in the middle of the damn lake, with a voice in the air and a crazy woman, and while he had so far retained some freedom of thought, he had no doubt that Ahnok could keep him from running away.

"Okay, as long as we're just talking temporary, I guess I can give you a ride off this island."

Ahnok didn't bother acknowledging Bradley's acquiescence. A column of mist rose up out of the black stone, whirled in the air for a few seconds, and then, like a swarm of wasps, flew straight at Bradley's head. His eyes went wide and he ducked his head to the side, but the swarm course corrected and the mist struck him full in the face. It tapered and two tendrils of mist entered his nostrils. At first he felt an icy chill in his nose, penetrating farther and farther up the nasal passage, and then he felt a shock like he'd touched a metal surface after scuffing his feet on a carpet, and his body shook like a bush in the wind.

Things went black for a flash, and then his mind was flooded with images as Ahnok's consciousness settled in. In that moment, Bradley knew that Ahnok had lied about almost everything. It had been *him* who had developed a blood lust. The others had put him away to protect the world and humanity from his growing thirst for violence and blood. Now, he was using Bradley to escape his prison, and his intent was to seek out his kindred and get his revenge. But, it was what he planned after that that sent chills through Bradley's mind. Mankind would not be able to defend itself against such as Ahnok. The world was a violent place, but with him running loose among mankind, the current violence would seem like a Sunday picnic.

Bradley pushed his hands against the earth and started to stand. As he came upright, he swayed, almost falling. He tried to fling his hands out for balance, but they wouldn't move.

Damn, I'm falling. Need to balance myself!

"Oh, I am sorry," Ahnok said. *"It has been a long time since I had corporeal form."* Bradley felt the control of his arms return just before he was about to plunge forward. He flung his arms out to regain his balance and slowly righted himself. *"Ah, I will leave the motivating to you, Bradley Matthews; at least until I have regained my ability to properly navigate in this form."*

"Thanks for small favors," Bradley said. "Now, what do we do?"

"We go to the boat and make our way off this cursed lake." Ahnok's resonate voice coming from his mouth, without the words having been processed through his brain, gave Bradley a creepy feeling.

But, he had control over his body now. That was something.

"Okay, let's go," he said, and started walking back the way he and Eve had come from the boat. "You coming, Eve?" he asked over his shoulder.

Stark followed him. A reverential gaze was on her face.

"Yes, master," she said.

Jeez, Bradley thought, *I wonder if that's for me or Ahnok.*

"It is for both of us, Bradley Matthews," Ahnok's voice sounded in his head. *"She finds you as impressive as I do."*

Oh, that's just great. I guess she'll be disappointed when I dump you after we get off this lake, huh?

214

"We shall see."

Bradley stifled the thought that was on the tip of his consciousness. No sense in letting this creep Ahnok know what he had in mind to do. He kept walking. The sound of Eve making her way through the thicket behind him was loud in the quiet night.

They made it to the boat in less time than it had taken to get from it to the clearing. Bradley held it steady to allow Eve to settle herself in the stern. He then pushed it into the water and stepped over the bow, careful not to let his feet touch the lake surface. Not yet. He grasped the oars and, following the instructions Eve had given him, turned the boat around and headed toward the shore.

"Okay, Eve," he said. "Give me directions to our first launch point."

She nodded, still smiling her vapid smile at him.

The sound of the oars splashing as they rose from the water lulled him. He felt his muscles burning from so much unaccustomed exercise, reminding himself that when this was all over he would have to get a gym membership. That was something Lena had bugged him about often when they first got married, and he'd promised he would, but never had.

His attention was suddenly drawn to the sounds of a commotion behind him. Looking back over his shoulder, he saw that they'd covered over half the distance from the island to the shore. On shore, he saw the crowd they'd left behind converging on two individuals, a man and a woman. He squinted. In the dim light he thought he recognized . . . no he *did* recognize them. It was Bill and Rebecca. What were they doing here? And, what were the people of Copper Cove doing to them?

He was too far away to tell exactly what was happening, but his gut told him that his friend and his boss were in trouble. It was time to act. Slowly, testing the limits of freedom he had, he grasped the sides of the boat and began to stand. Eve's eyes went wide.

"W-what are you doing, Bradley?" she asked through trembling lips.

"I just want to get a better look at what's happening over there," he said, pulling himself fully upright with his feet shoulder width apart.

"We have unwelcome visitors," Ahnok said. Bradley still found it strange to have his lips moving and someone else's voice coming from his mouth. *"I am instructing the community in how to take care of them."*

Oh, no you don't! Bradley's mind fairly screamed the thought. He brought his feet together and leaned to his left.

"Bradley, no!" Eve shouted. "You will fall out of the boat!"

Ahnok's attention had been distracted by the scene on the lake shore, but when Stark shouted, he probed deep into Bradley's mind and saw what he intended; what he was in fact in the process of doing.

"No, Bradley Matthews," he said. *"It will not be that easy."*

But it was, in fact, just that easy.

Bradley had laid his plan around the fact that Ahnok's rustiness in manipulating a physical form would slow him down. He'd noticed also that the spirit—he no longer had a problem acknowledging that—had limits. When he was controlling a large group, his control of Bradley was limited.

He was using the law of gravity against a being accustomed to having things his, its, own way. A being totally unprepared for a human who did not look upon it with awe; and one prepared to do battle.

Bradley was already precariously off-balance, and he could feel himself falling. Ahnok could obviously feel the same sensation. As Bradley anticipated he would, Ahnok seized control of his arms, and as Bradley had done when he was in danger of falling in the clearing, he flung them out to the sides. And, that was his undoing.

The motion of his arms, added to the weight of his upper body, already being pulled downward by gravity, only accelerated Bradley's fall. He felt his outer left calf strike the sharp edge of the boat's side, sending a spark of pain up his leg. As he continued his fall toward the dark water of the lake, he heard Eve's shrill scream, "No, Bradley, no!" Then, he heard Ahnok's voice, inside his head and issuing from his mouth,

"No-o-o-o-o-o-o-o-o-o!"

His head hit the water first. The cold of the water sent shock waves through his body. Weight and momentum pulled him downward. The dark water slid past his open eyes. Time, he discovered, is not a fixed concept, but fluid depending upon what is being experienced. Some things seem to fly by, while others float like dandelion spores in a gentle breeze. Bradley's perception was fragmented, and time moved slowly. He heard Eve's screaming. He heard Ahnok's screams coming from his own mouth until his head was completely submerged, and the cold water of the lake rushed into his mouth and down his throat, turning Ahnok's screams into unintelligible gurgles. He could feel, just for a moment, Ahnok's efforts to control his outstretched arms; to force him to grab for the boat. But, the effort was fleeting. He willed his arms to hang loosely as his body, head down at first, and then gradually rotating until he was sinking feet first into the darkness below him.

` *"You cannot do this,"* Ahnok's voice boomed within his skull, but there was a note of panic in it. *"You will die!"*

And, so will you, thought Bradley, *and, so will you*.

Then, time stopped.

Bradley felt a white hot pain tearing through his body, beginning in his chest and ripping out through the top of his skull. He sensed rather than saw a bright flash. A sizzling sound echoed in his ears.

And then, things went black.

Charles Ray

CHAPTER 30

The people standing at the edge of the lake were focused on something out on the water, so, at first, they didn't notice as William and Rebecca Davis drew near. But, a portly man in a three-piece suit at the back of the crowd turned and saw them.

"We have company," he said in a startled voice, and tapped the shoulder of the man in front of him.

They froze in place. The crowd turned as one, all eyes on the newcomers. A man dressed in a brown uniform with a shiny badge over his left breast pocket stepped forward.

"Who are you and what are you doing here?" he asked.

William scanned the crowd. The man in brown, some kind of cop, didn't seem particularly threatening, despite the stern tone in his question. Next to him was a man wearing coveralls who had a quizzical look on his sun darkened face. Behind these two was a shorter fat man with slightly stooped shoulders who had a definitely hostile expression on *his* face, but the rest of the people whose faces he could see in the mass just seemed curious. Nonetheless, he and Davis were interlopers here, and he didn't want to antagonize them until he knew more about what was going on.

"Hi, my name is William Lewis, and this is Professor Rebecca Davis," he said. "We think our friend Bradley Matthews might be here in your town. We're looking for him."

The two men exchanged glances. "Bradley Matthews? Never heard of him," the man in brown said.

William knew instantly that the man was lying. But, it was Davis who stepped forward. She fixed the man with a glacial stare.

"You sure about that . . . officer?" she asked. "I detected a flicker of recognition on your face when you heard his name."

William could picture her facing down a student with that glare and tone of voice. The man leaned away from her, his eyes flicking right and left. He quickly straightened and put his hands on his hips. He put a stern expression on his face, but Davis continued to stare him down.

"I am sorry, I do not know what you are talking about, but you should watch your tone of voice," he said. "I am the sheriff here in Copper Cove, and I know everyone here. We do not have anyone named Bradley Matthews here, so I suggest that the two of you turn around and leave."

Despite the stern expression, the way his eyes darted around and his lip quivered, he wasn't pulling it off very well. William could see that Davis wasn't buying it either. She had her hands on her hips and leaned forward, frowning at the lawman. William eased forward, putting his shoulder partially in front of her.

"Look, sheriff," he said. "Nothing personal, but I agree with Professor Davis. Just as we were driving into town, I saw Bradley walking in front of you people. Didn't you hear the horn blowing?"

The sheriff's face creased and his eye movements increased. He looked to be on the verge of breaking down. That was sufficient proof in William's mind that he was hiding something. In his experience, cops *never* backed down in confrontations with civilians.

"Y-you must be mistaken," the man said. "There were no strangers with us on our journey here to the lake."

"I don't think so," Davis said.

William agreed with her. The man seemed to be truthful about there being no strangers, but he was *sure* he'd seen Bradley.

The man who had been frowning from the crowd stepped forward. "There is no point trying to reason with them, Jason. They know," he said. "We must detain them until Ahnok arrives. He can decide what to do with them."

The crowd started moving forward. William put an arm across in front of Davis, pushing her backward.

"I don't like the looks of this, Rebecca," he said.

"What do we do?" she asked. There was a tiny tremor in her voice.

"We run like hell, is what we do."

William spun around, grabbed Davis's shoulder and shoved her forward. She stumbled, caught her balance and began pumping her long legs. He followed quickly after her. He could hear the thump of feet on the soft earth behind him.

"Get them?" a male voice shouted.

"Cully, you and Philo cut over by the church," the sheriff's voice called. "Cut them off before they get back to town."

Suddenly, there was a scream, a high-pitched keening from far behind them. The footsteps stopped, and so did William. Davis kept running for a few more feet before she, too, stopped.

"What's going on?" she asked.

"I don't know," he said. "I think I heard a woman scream. Sounded like it came from the lake. Maybe someone fell in."

Their pursuers had also stopped and turned toward the lake. One by one, slowly at first, and then gradually coming to a jog, they started back toward the lake. Curious, William followed.

The scream sounded again, followed by a man's voice, "No-o-o-o-o-o—", which was suddenly cut off, and followed by a loud roar and a flash of light like lightning striking nearby. Blinded by the flash, William felt a pressure like someone running into him full tilt, or like being hit by a well thrown ball as he had been many times while playing dodge ball in junior high school, and his body was lifted from the ground.

Mercifully, he was unconscious before his body crashed to earth.

Charles Ray

CHAPTER 31

His lungs felt like they were on fire. When he opened his eyes, all he could see was a dark, blurry, undulating grey curtain, and he was floating in some kind of liquid. He opened his mouth, and felt water pouring in and down his throat, and saw bubbles floating past his eyes. He snapped his mouth shut. All of this took place in a couple of seconds, but to Bradley it felt like an eternity. Worse, for that first two seconds, only those portions of his brain that controlled autonomous functions seemed to be working. When the cognitive parts kicked in, he first realized where he was—underwater and sinking fast—then, he remembered how he'd gotten here. Next, the will to survive kicked in, and he began kicking with his feet and clawing upwards with his hands. He clamped his mouth shut and fought the urge to breathe.

His time in the orphanage and in successive foster homes had never afforded him the opportunity to learn to swim, and in college, after meeting Lena and William, he'd just never bothered. But, one of the strongest drives of any living creature is the will to survive. Babies are born with the ability to swim. When faced with the prospect of drowning, Bradley's lizard brain took over. It felt like it was taking forever, and the rational part of his brain kept trying to tell him to relax and let the darkness take over; that he couldn't make it. His lungs felt like they would burst, and every muscle in his body was on fire. But, just when he thought he'd reached the end of his reserves, he heard Lena's voice, *"You can do this, Bradley. It's not your time to die. Live, my darling, live for me."*

That gave him the push he needed. He pulled hard with his arms, and kicked his feet, and . . . the water was running down his face, and his vision was no longer blurred. He could see the boat floating on the surface of the lake a few feet in front of him. He flailed at the water, dog paddling toward the boat. A few strokes brought him close enough to be able to grasp the side. He pulled himself to the side, and rested his forehead against the rough wood, taking in air in huge gasps. As he breathed in a dank, acidic smell assaulted his nostrils. It seemed to be coming from the boat primarily, but wafted in from the shore as well.

When the feeling had come back into his arms and his breathing had steadied, he pulled himself up until his chest pressed against the top of the boat rail. He expected to see an angry Eve Stark in the boat. Instead, all he saw in the stern of the craft was a pile of smoldering ash—the source of the unpleasant odor. Holding his breath, he heaved himself over the side and into the boat. He tried to ignore the pile of ash as he rowed toward the shore.

By the time the bow of the boat plowed into the mushy ground at the lake's edge, Bradley's arms were aching from the effort. He scrambled up and climbed over the bow, stumbling and falling to his knees in the soft earth. He knelt there for a full minute, catching his breath and letting the throbbing in his arms, shoulder and back subside. When he felt he could stand without tumbling over, he stood and looked around.

Twenty yards from the edge of the lake, in the light of the moon, he saw several piles of smoldering ash. Beyond that he saw two shapes about twenty feet apart that after blinking to clear his vision he recognized as bodies. He rushed toward the nearest.

When he came to it, he instantly recognized—his friend, William. He knelt near the body, feeling for a pulse. He found one, weak, but steady. He felt the arms and legs, looking for broken bones. As he patted

William's arm, the man moaned and his eyelids fluttered.

"Bill, Bill," Bradley said. "Are you okay? What happened?" He patted his friend's wrist as he spoke.

Finally, after a few more flutters of his lids, William opened his eyes. He looked up with an unfocused stare, shaking his head.

"Wha-, what happened?" His voice was weak and shaky. "W-where's Rebecca?"

Bradley looked toward the other body. He realized who it must be.

"Wait here, Bill. Don't move," he said. "I'll check."

Rising swiftly, he ran the ten feet to where Rebecca Davis lay. She writhed on the ground, rubbing at her eyes.

"What's going on?" she asked weakly. "W-what happened?"

Bradley knelt next to her, cradling her head, he helped her to a sitting position.

"Are you okay?" he asked.

She shook her head, but said, "I think so. Doesn't feel like anything's broken, but I have a hell of a headache." She looked up at him and blinked. "Where did you come from?"

"I was on the lake," he said. "There was a flash and a bang and I got tossed into the water. When I got back into the boat and rowed ashore, I found Bill . . . and you. What happened?"

"I'm not sure," she said. "William and I were talking to the people near the lake, and they suddenly turned unfriendly. We were running away when there was a scream. We turned around, and there was a flash and a . . . I don't know, some kind of bang, and I was knocked out. Where's William? Is he okay?"

"Yeah, he's just over there. He apparently got knocked down too. Can you stand?"

She swayed a bit. He grasped her shoulders tighter. "Uh, yeah, I think so." She started to rise. He helped her. She swayed slightly, but finally shook herself and squared her shoulders. "I'm okay," she said. "Let's check on William."

They walked over to where William was sitting up, his heads in his hands. Davis rushed over and knelt next to him, pulling his head to her breasts.

"Are you okay?" she asked.

Bradley had never heard such tenderness in her voice before.

"I . . . think so," William said. "What the hell happened?"

"I don't know. William, Bradley's here."

William twisted his head around. "Hey, bro," he said. "You okay. What's going on? Where are those crazy people who were chasing us?"

They then took in the fact that Bradley's clothing was soaking wet.

"Hey, dude," William said. "Why are you all wet?"

Bradley brushed at his wet clothing, and tried to sort an answer out in his mind.

"First, let's get back to town and your car," he said. "I'll tell you what I know, and you're gonna think I'm crazy."

CHAPTER 32

"What do you mean everyone's gone?"
Lewis asked. "How could they all be gone?"

Bradley had explained that the entire town's population, nearly two hundred people had somehow vanished into thin air. He left out the part about the piles of ash, which Lewis and Davis hadn't noticed in the dark. A whole town disappearing was, he thought, about all their traumatized minds would be able to process.

They were standing near the worn shell of a building, its timbers grey with age and with the rusted iron skeleton of a roof, pitted and covered with green mold. Inside sat Bradley's Jeep. Next to it was a rusted Model T, what was left of its tires were black and grey tatters of rubber, and its metal was rusted through. It had once been black, but was now a red and brown rusted hulk. The remains of other vehicles, horse-drawn two-wheeled carriages, now mere piles of rubble, were scattered about over the dirt floor of what had once been some kind of garage or repair facility. Strangely, he noticed that his duffle bag, rather than being in the room he occupied in the now derelict inn, was on the back seat where he'd put it just before leaving Washington.

The rest of the town was in a similar state of decay and decrepitude. The street that ran through its center was a jumble of pitted concrete, some slabs tilting up at odd angles, with grass growing in large cracks that crisscrossed like a jigsaw puzzle that had been tossed negligently upon a table. The buildings, what few were still standing, were rotted out hulks, with gaps where windows once were. The sides were grey and peeling and covered with the same green mold as the building containing the vehicles.

"And, what happened to the town?" Davis asked with wonder in her voice. "It didn't look like this when we drove in."

"I think this Ahnok character must have created some kind of mass hypnosis," Bradley said. "He made us believe the town was occupied, but when he . . . I mean, I went into the water it broke the spell."

William laughed. "Man, do you hear yourself? Do you actually believe that?"

"You got a better explanation?" William looked down and shrugged. "Right, that's what I thought. Besides, you and Professor

Davis . . . Rebecca saw a crowd of people in a town that was clearly populated and functioning when you arrived, right?"

"Uh, yeah, I guess we did."

"So, that supports my theory," Bradley said. "This guy . . . thing . . . was inside my head for just a short period, and it was such a shock I don't remember much, but I shared his memories, and what I saw was amazing." He paused to gather his thoughts. "He was old; and I mean ancient. He and his kind were here before humans. They came right after the dinosaurs, but before humans."

"Do you think they came from . . ." Rebecca Davis pointed up at the sky.

Bradley gazed up at the darkening sky.

"That makes as much sense as anything. Anyway, Ahnok was part of a group of four, and when humans came, especially the first European explorers and settlers, he developed a taste for human violence and bloodshed, so his . . . he called them kindred . . . exiled him to that island in the lake as punishment. He'd been there for nearly three hundred years."

"Damn! You mean this town's been here that long and no one knew about it?" Lewis said. "How can that be?"

"I didn't get deep enough in his mind to figure that one out. But hell, he was able to block my phone signal." He took his phone out and held it up so they could see. The signal indicator showed five bars. "And, he made this rundown old ghost town look like it was alive and functioning. So, I figure he must have had some kind of ability to cloak the town to keep people from noticing it unless he wanted them to."

"So," William said. "That argues for him being an ET, doesn't it?"

"Or, he could be an ancient god," Davis added.

Bradley shrugged. "Who knows? Could be either, or it could just be some dude with some powerful drugs that induce mass hypnosis."

"Yeah, how does that explain the fact that we were in the car when we saw the town and the people," William said in a peevish tone. "We hadn't done any drugs."

"It could have been dispersed in the air, and you breathed it in through the car's ventilator system."

William shook his head. "But, your car's parked in that pile of rubble over there, next to those other rusted hulks. It's still got your shit inside, and you been here two days. Where've you been sleeping? And, don't tell me on the ground, you're too neat for that."

"I can't explain it," Bradley said. "Maybe I slept in my car. I don't know."

William shook his head. "It's all too much to process. This is like some wild ass science fiction movie, or that *Alien* movie, and I'm half expecting some ugly monster to pop up at any minute."

They all looked around, but nothing stirred but a mini-whirlwind that meandered down the middle of the torn up street tossing leaves and dust in its wake. It was full on dark. Bradley glanced at his watch. The luminous green numerals stood at 8:45. He realized that it was the first time he'd looked at his watch since his car stopped running out on Highway 4.

The whole thing seemed so unreal. Had it, in fact, been real? If his best friend hadn't been standing there, close enough to touch, and his boss, Rebecca Davis beside him, he would have concluded that he'd just woken from a hallucinogenic episode. His mind spun.

Rebecca Davis brought everyone back to reality. "So, fellows," she said in her best lecture hall tone of voice. "What do we do now? We can't tell anyone about this, because if we did, they'd immediately lock us away in a padded room." She looked at Bradley. "Neither you nor I need something like this on our record if we wish to continue working at a conservative institution like Georgetown."

William nodded vigorously. "That's for sure. And, the guys I work for would drop me like a sack of dog poop if I turned up telling this story."

"So," Bradley said. "You two are saying that we just forget that any of this happened?"

"You got a better idea?" William put a hand on his shoulder and squeezed.

Bradley's shoulder slumped in defeat. "No, I guess not."

"So, again I ask, what do we do now?" Davis asked.

"I think I'm going to drive on to Chesapeake Beach like I planned," Bradley said. "I made a promise to Lena and I plan to keep it. I suppose you two should just drive on back to DC."

Davis stepped between them and placed hands on both men's shoulders. She smiled at Bradley, but when she turned to look at William, Bradley saw her smile warm up several degrees.

"It's late, and we're closer to Chesapeake Beach than DC," she said. "I think we should all go there, find rooms and get some rest." She gently squeezed Bradley's shoulder. "And, if you don't mind, I'd like to join you when you say farewell to Lena. I only met her briefly, but I really liked her."

"I'd like to be there, too," William said softly.

Bradley felt the sting of salty tears and a warm feeling in his chest that he hadn't felt in a long time.

"You know, I think Lena would like that," he said.

CHAPTER 33

After retrieving Bradley's Jeep, they set out for Highway 4 with him leading and William riding with Davis in her car. The road, which had seemed like a well-maintained blacktop when Bradley first saw it, was little more than parallel tire tracks in the grass, with no sign of frequent or recent traffic other than their two vehicles. At the highway, he noticed that the sign indicating Copper Cove was nearly covered by a tangle of vines and was so weather-worn and faded it would be almost impossible to read from a vehicle passing on the highway at normal speed. He looked in the rearview mirror. Behind Davis's car, the forest that surrounded Copper Cove looked like giant sentinels, or monsters guarding some ancient fortress He took a deep breath, put the Jeep in gear and stepped on the accelerator, turning the wheel left when he felt the tires on concrete for the drive to Chesapeake Beach.

They arrived at the bayside town just after 10:30 pm. Luckily they were able to get two rooms in the same bed and breakfast that Bradley and Lena had stayed in. The clerk had given Bradley and William keys to one room on the second floor, and Davis a key to another on the third, assuming the two men would room together. They said nothing until they were at the door to the second floor room. Davis gave William a look, and he smiled at Bradley and trailed off after her as she headed toward the stairs. Bradley could only smile and shake his head. Despite the difference in their ages, the two seemed a good fit, and it was good to see his friend taking an interest in a woman of substance instead of the bar hopping coeds he usually chased.

Bradley slept peacefully that night, and was up the next morning before sunrise. He had nearly finished his breakfast before Davis and William joined him. They both wore smiles of satisfaction, overlaid with a tinge of embarrassment, which caused him to smile broadly, further embarrassing them.

By the time they'd finished breakfast and walked to the shore of the bay a few hundred yards south of the wharf, they were more comfortable with the situation, and Davis walked with her arm linked in William's and her head on his shoulder. Bradley carried the urn containing Lena's ashes, cradling it against his chest. They found a tiny, white sand beach, ringed on the land side by tall saw grass, and relatively secluded. A gentle breeze was blowing from north to south, creating little whitecaps on the bay's dark blue surface. Off to the east, the sky was just turning pink.

"I remember this beach," Bradley said. "Lena and I walked here and watched the sun rise one day."

"It's beautiful," said Davis. "So peaceful."

"The perfect spot," agreed William.

Nodding, Bradley removed the cover of the urn and held it up as he faced the rising sun. "Lena Nelson Matthews," he said as tears streaked down his brown cheeks. "I give you the sun, I give you the sea, and I give you the earth. This is a place where we knew love and peace. May you have eternal love and peace."

He tilted the urn. The fine grey ash drifted from the opening, and, caught by the wind, swirled out in a streamer catching the rays of the rising sun and glinting like fireflies. Most of the ashes settled on the water, while some drifted gently down onto the sand and down in the grass.

"Shuck," William said. "Not all of it made it into the water."

"That's okay. She would have wanted it that way," Bradley said. "Now, she is part of both."

They stood there, watching the sun slowly ascend into a sky now turning bright blue, with Rebecca between them, her arms around both. From a distance they looked like a family enjoying an early morning sunset.

CHAPTER 34

As the sun rose into the blue sky, casting long shadows in the forest of old, gnarled trees, a bundle of rags at the base of one particularly old and twisted oak began to stir. Harry Paxton stared up through the canopy of leaves through rheumy eyes at the blotches of sky. He heard the muted sound of bird calls. His joints ached from having lain on the damp ground all night.

Slowly and painfully, using the bole of the tree for support, he pulled himself to an upright position; or as upright as he could manage with his curved spine and arthritic joints.

His body was failing, but his mind was still sharp. His memory was good too. Of course, keeping over a hundred years of memories straight wasn't an easy task. He could, though, remember the important things. He remembered, for instance, driving along the highway in his brand new Model T Ford, fresh from the factory in Detroit, when it stopped running right there at the intersection with that road heading off east into the forest. He remembered the sheriff, a young fellow, name of Jason Warfield, riding up on an old bay and offering to help out. He'd let Harry ride behind him back to the town, a little one-horse burg back in the woods, and had sent the livery man, Philo, out with a team of horses to tow his car in to the livery stable for repairs. Philo had told him they'd have to send off to Baltimore for the parts, so they arranged for him to stay at the inn. He smiled, an open mouth grin that showed more spaces than brown and crooked teeth, as he remembered the woman who ran the place. Eve Stark. Now, that was one fine woman. And, she took a shine to him right away. Pretty soon, he didn't care how long the repairs to his car were going to take. Then, it was too late.

He'd never been sure what happened. Maybe Eve had put something in his food or drink. Maybe he'd fallen in love. In lust was actually more like it, he remembered fondly. There'd been a few other lovelies in the town who'd taken a liking to him. He never went to bed alone after the second night.

For a drifter like Harry Paxton, a traveling purveyor of cheap household appliances who usually sold just enough to keep himself in whiskey and cigarettes, having an unlimited supply of food, wine, and women was like dying and going to heaven. He fancied himself a sultan, and Copper Cove was his kingdom with a varied and willing harem. At first, he found it strange that the other men in town showed no signs of jealousy, but then he came to accept it. It wasn't until a long time afterwards, how long he couldn't remember, as days melted into weeks into months into years, and he'd lost complete track of time, that he realized that there was something else. That it wasn't something in his food or drink, or the hedonistic pleasures that bound him to Copper Cove. It was literally something in the water. Something in the lake.

Now, Harry Paxton, in addition to being a wandering traveling salesman, was insatiably curious. He'd never seen a puzzle he didn't try to solve. So, when he surmised that the secret of Copper Cove lay in the lake, he'd set out to get to the bottom of it.

He'd found a boat and was just about to shove it into the water when he felt a force pushing him away from the water's edge, and a voice in his head warning him to stay away from the lake.

Harry wasn't a superstitious man. He didn't believe in ghosts. He wasn't particularly religious. But, that force and that voice, well, they put the fear of God . . . no, the fear of the Devil into him. He wandered back to town and resumed the life that was now all he had. But, he'd also changed. He seemed distant and disconnected from what was going on around him. He was no longer pleased at his circumstance. His harem lost its allure. And, he began to lose his mind.

He hung in for a few more years, until one day, he simply wandered into the woods. From that day on he became the old mad man of the forest. Food would be left for him at the old church, but no one would speak to him or even look at him. No one until the day the young colored guy had followed him.

That encounter had snapped something loose in his head. Had opened the curtain that had been thrown across his memory, bringing forth images that had been only dimly perceived for so many years.

And, with the memories came the voice. He hadn't realized it, but he'd missed the voice.

"Harry, I need you," the voice said.

He recognized it. It was the voice of the Devil. And, the Devil needed old Harry again.

"Yes, Harry, I need you. Come to me. Come to the lake."

With a smile on his craggy face, Harry Paxton turned toward the lake and in a shuffling, shambling gait put one foot in front of the other.

"I'm coming, master," he croaked.

EPILOGUE

The thing that bothered him most was the darkness.

After that was the sense of betrayal; the ancient betrayal of his kindred, the treacherous bastards who had exiled him on that tiny spit of land in the middle of that fetid body of water, and then, most humiliating of all, that insufferable human who had tricked him, and almost, almost destroyed him.

Had he not been distracted by the untimely arrival of the strangers, and the need to mobilize the townspeople to take care of them, it would never have happened. Never before had a mere mortal bettered him, and never again.

He hadn't noticed at first when the fool started falling, mistaking it for the boat rocking. By the time he realized what was happening, the only thing he could think of doing was move the arms to try and regain his . . . the mortal's . . . balance. But, it had been so long since he'd manipulated a physical body, he'd miscalculated, and his actions had actually aided in what the damned sack of flesh was trying to do. He'd caused the fall to speed up, sending Matthews into the dark, dangerous water. Then, he'd compounded his error by screaming, an action that opened the mortal's mouth and allowed the water to pour in.

Never before had he felt such pain. There had been the pain when his treacherous kindred had wrenched him from the mortal shell he'd occupied, after dragging him to the island in the middle of the lake. But, as bad as that had been, it was a pinprick compared to the feeling when the first droplets of that poisonous combination of hydrogen and oxygen in liquid form lapped at the edge of his being. For a moment he felt as if he was being torn apart.

But, the instinct for survival, high in mortals, is even higher for those who are as close to immortal as can be attained without attaining godhood. He knew that staying within the mortal shell was tantamount to extinction. In nanoseconds he weighed his options, and discovered only one. It would be a close thing, and would require exquisite timing, something that only a being of his ability could achieve.

He shrunk his essence into the tiniest space he could manage, as far away from the passages that were rapidly filling with water *as possible, and when the mortal was only a few meters from the silty bottom of the lake, he'd separated from him, aiming straight down, and moving as fast as possible in his weakened state, a state that still left him with more energy than any mortal could hope to have, he'd bored down toward the silt, penetrating it like a laser through paper, diving deeper until he was beyond the silt, through the underlying bedrock, only stopping when he sensed the immense heat of the planet's core a few thousand kilometers farther on.*

Only then did he stop. He was within a cavern of the rock making up the planet's mantle; that layer of hot, semi-solid rock, nearly 3,000 kilometers thick. He'd penetrated about halfway through, far enough from the crust to avoid water from the surface reaching him, but not so close to the hot liquid outer core. He was safe for now.

Safe, but not satisfied. He'd failed in his mission. Foiled by a mere mortal. His kindred would once more go unpunished for the indignity they'd heaped upon him. But, Ahnok was patient above all. His time would come. They would pay. First, though, he would have to find and punish the mortal. Bradley Matthews must die. The question that swirled around in that portion of his energy field that in a mortal would be called a brain was, how? He could go back to the surface, but without a mortal shell to protect him from exposure to water, it would be dangerous.

He needed another vehicle. Unfortunately, at the moment of separation from the mortal, he'd loosened his hold on the avatars of the place the mortals called Copper Cove, the only thing that had held them together for nearly three centuries. Even as he fled, he sensed their dissolution. For all his power, he could not bring them back. They were now dust upon the wind.

From deep within the earth he sent out his sensory probes, sensing nothing at first. They were gone, back to the dust from whence they came. He sensed Matthews and the other two, faint and becoming fainter as they moved beyond the range of his sensory ability, adding to his anger and frustration. Then, just before he pulled back to contemplate his next move, he felt it. Faint, but growing in strength as it moved closer and closer to the lake.

He reached out, and felt it. A flicker of consciousness. Not what he would have considered a worthy vessel, but a human. There was something familiar about it, like a food that has not been tasted in a long time, but the memory of which still lingers in memory. Slowly, like treacle on a cold morning, the memory crystallized. The old one. The one who had been cast off long before. Rejected by Ahnok and treated as an outcast by his avatars.

Not the best choice. During a better time, not a choice at all.

"But," Ahnok mused to himself. "Beggars cannot be choosers."

Charles Ray

Other books by this author:

Al Pennyback mysteries
Color Me Dead
Memorial to the Dead
Deadline
Dead, White, and Blue
A Good Day to Die
The Day the Music Died
Die, Sinner
Deadly Intentions
Death by Design
Till Death Do Us Part
Deadly Dose
Dead Man's Cove
Dead Men Don't Answer
Deadly Paradise
Kiss of Death
Death in White Satin
Death and Taxis
Deadbeat
A Deadly Wind Blows
Death Wish
Deadly Vendetta
A Time to Kill, A Time to Die
Dead Ringer

Ed Lazenby mystery
Butterfly Effect

The Buffalo Soldier series:

Buffalo Soldier: Trial by Fire
Buffalo Soldier: Homecoming
Buffalo Soldier: Incident at Cactus Junction
Buffalo Soldier: Peacekeepers
Buffalo Soldier: Renegade
Buffalo Soldier: Escort Duty
Buffalo Soldier: Battle at Dead Man's Gulch
Buffalo Soldier: Yosemite
Buffalo Soldier: Comanchero
Buffalo Soldier: Range War
Buffalo Soldier: Mob Justice
Buffalo Soldier: Chasing Ghosts

Other fiction

Angel on His Shoulder
She's No Angel
Child of the Flame
Pip's Revenge
Here, There Be Demons
Wallace in Underland
Further Adventures of Wallace in Underland
Dead Letter and Other Tales
The White Dragons
The Dragon's Lair
Dragon Slayer
The Last Gunfighters
The Culling
Frontier Justice: Bass Reeves, Deputy
  U.S. Marshal
Angel on His Shoulder-Revised Edition

Battle at the Galactic Junkyard
Mountain Man
Devil's Lake

Nonfiction

*Things I Learned from My Grandmother About
    Leadership and Life*
*Taking Charge: Effective Leadership for the
    Twenty-first Century*
Grab the Brass ring
*African Places: A Photographic Journey
    Through Zimbabwe and southern Africa*
A Portrait of Africa
There's Always a Plan B
*In the Line of Fire: American Diplomats in
    the Trenches*
Advice for the Insecure Writer
Looking at Life Through My Lens

Children's books

The Yak and the Yeti
Samantha and the Bully
Molly Learns to Share
Where is Teddy?
Catie and Mister Hop-Hop

See these and other books by this author at:
http://www.amazon.com/Charles-
Ray/e/B006WMLEZK

Charles Ray

About the Author

Charles Ray has been writing fiction since his teens. He won a Sunday school magazine writing contest when he was thirteen, and having his byline on a short story published in a national publication forever hooked him on writing. During his time in the army (1962-1982) he often moonlighted as a newspaper or magazine journalist, and was the editorial cartoonist for the Spring Lake (NC) News, a weekly newspaper, during the 1970s. In addition to his writing, he was an artist/cartoonist and photographer for a number of publications, including Ebony, Eagle and Swan, and Essence, and had a monthly cartoon feature and did several covers for Buffalo, a now-defunct magazine that was dedicated to showcasing the contributions of African-Americans to the country's military history.

After retiring from the army, he joined the U.S. Foreign Service, and served as a diplomat in posts in Asia and Africa until his retirement in 2012. He has worked and traveled throughout the world (Antarctica is the only continent he hasn't visited), and now, as a full time writer, continues to globetrot looking for interesting things to write about, draw, or take pictures of.

A native of Texas, he now calls Maryland

home. For more on his writing and other projects, check one of the following Web sites:

http://charlesaray.blogspot.com
http://charlieray45.wordpress.com
http://www.twitter.com/charlieray45
http://www.facebook.com/charlieray45
http://www.flickr.com/photos/charlesray45/
http://www.viewbug.com/member/charlesray

www.ingramcontent.com/pod-product-compliance
Lightning Source LLC
Chambersburg PA
CBHW071458170626
46811CB00007B/2625